New Beginnings

RACHEL YODER—
Always Trouble Somewhere

Book 4

WANDA &
BRUNSTETTER

BARBOUR
PUBLISHING

ISBN 978-1-59789-898-0

All Pennsylvania Dutch words are taken from the *Revised Pennsylvania German Dictionary* found in Lancaster County, Pennsylvania.

Scripture taken from the HOLY BIBLE, NEW INTERNATIONAL VERSION®. NIV®. Copyright © 1973, 1978, 1984 by International Bible Society. Used by permission of Zondervan. All rights reserved.

Cover artist: Richard Hoit

For more information about Wanda E. Brunstetter, please access the author's Web site at the following Internet address: www.wandabrunstetter.com

This book is a work of fiction. Names, characters, places, and incidents are either products of the author's imagination or used fictitiously. Any similarity to actual people, organizations, and/or events is purely coincidental.

Published by Barbour Publishing, Inc., P.O. Box 719, Uhrichsville, Ohio 44683, www.barbourbooks.com

Our mission is to publish and distribute inspirational products offering exceptional value and biblical encouragement to the masses.

Member of the
Evangelical Christian
Publishers Association

Printed in the United States of America.

Dedication

To the students and teachers at the Pleasant Ridge School in Shipshewana, Indiana. Thanks for letting me visit with you!

Glossary

ach—oh
bensel—silly child
boppli—baby
bruder—brother
danki—thank you
daed—dad
dochder—daughter
dumm—dumb
gaul—horse
gemmummelt—mumbling
grossdaadi—grandfather
grossmudder—grandmother
gut nacht—good night
hochmut—pride
jah—yes
kapp—cap
kichlin—cookies
kinner—children
kumme—come
lecherich—ridiculous
mamm—mom
midder—mothers
millich—milk
mudich—spirited
mupsich—stupid
naas—nose
naerfich—nervous
narrisch—crazy
reider—rider
rutschich—squirming

schmaert—smart
schnell—quickly
schpeckmaus—bat
schweschder—sister
verhuddelt—mixed up
wunderbaar—wonderful

Duh die katz naus.—Put the cat out.
En aldi grauns.—An old grumbler.
Es dutt mir leed.—I am sorry.
Fege.—Run about.
Kanscht seller gaul reide?—Are you able to ride that horse?
Schpiele gern.—Like to play.
Was fehlt dir denn?—What's the matter with you?
Was is do uff?—What's the matter here?
Wie geht's?—How are you?

Contents

Chapter 1
Saying Good-bye

Plunk! Plunk! Plunk! Plunk! Ten-year-old Rachel Yoder dropped four dirty spoons into the sink full of soapy water. Mom had gone outside to hang some laundry on the clothesline and left Rachel to wash the dishes. Doing dishes was not one of Rachel's favorite things to do on a sunny spring morning. She'd much rather be outside playing with her cat, Cuddles; riding on her skateboard in the barn; petting their old horse, Tom; or looking at the colorful flowers blooming in Mom's flowerbeds.

Rachel looked out the kitchen window and spotted Grandpa Schrock working in the garden. Even pulling weeds would be better than doing dishes!

At least I have two hands I can use to do the dishes, Rachel thought. When she'd broken her arm a few months ago, she'd learned to do some things using only one hand. She was glad her arm had healed and she didn't have to wear the uncomfortable cast anymore. And she was glad this was Saturday and she could go outside to play after the dishes were done.

On the other side of the yard she saw Pap and her seventeen-year-old brother, Henry. They were building a dog run for her brother Jacob's dog. Jacob was twelve years old and was sometimes nice to Rachel, but most of the time he just picked on her. Now that spring was here and the snow had melted, Pap decided it was time to get Buddy out of the empty stall in the barn. The big, shaggy, red dog had slept there since Orlie Troyer gave him to Jacob a few months ago.

Buddy had been nothing but trouble ever since he'd come to live at their place. Rachel thought he deserved to be locked up. During the winter, when Jacob kept Buddy in the empty stall, Buddy jumped over the door and escaped several times. Rachel was glad the hairy mutt wouldn't be able to escape from his new dog run with a sturdy wire fence around it.

Rachel washed all the silverware and looked out the window again. She saw Jacob step out of the barn. Buddy was at his side, wagging his tail and nudging Jacob's hand with his nose.

Rachel frowned as she thought of all the times Buddy had licked her hand or face with his big slimy tongue.

Swish! Swish! Rachel ran the sponge over one of their breakfast plates as she continued to stare out the window, where she saw Buddy and Jacob in the backyard, playing with a ball.

Jacob tossed the ball across the yard, and Buddy

raced after it. Jacob clapped his hands to call Buddy back, but Buddy didn't come. Instead he rolled the ball with his nose, and then he took off in the opposite direction. Jacob sprinted after the dog, hollering and waving his hands.

Rachel grunted. "*Mupsich* [stupid] dog never does come when you call him." She thought about the whistle Jacob bought so he could train Buddy. But blowing the whistle never made the dog come when he was called. Buddy had a mind of his own. Rachel didn't think he could ever be trained.

She sloshed another dish around in the soapy water, rinsed it, and placed it in the dish drainer. *I hope Cuddles isn't in the yard right now. If Buddy sees my cat, he'll probably forget about the ball and start chasing after her.*

Rachel grabbed the frying pan Mom had used to make scrambled eggs for breakfast and dropped it into the soapy water. *Woosh!*—several bubbles floated into the air. One landed on Rachel's nose. *Pop!* She giggled and wiped it away then started scrubbing the frying pan.

The rumble of buggy wheels and the *clip-clop* of a horse's hooves pulled Rachel's gaze back to the window. When the horse and buggy came to a stop near the barn, Uncle Ben stepped down, followed by Aunt Irma, and Rachel's cousins—Mary, Nancy, Abe, and Sam.

Rachel saw Mom drop a towel into the laundry basket and hurry over to greet them. Grandpa set his shovel aside and headed toward Uncle Ben's buggy. Pap and Henry put their tools down and joined them. Jacob stopped chasing after Buddy and headed that way, too.

Rachel scoured the frying pan once more and quickly dried it and her hands before putting it away. Then she flung open the back door and raced outside. "What a surprise! I didn't know you were coming over today!" she called to Mary.

Woof! Woof! Buddy raced around the side of the house, leaped into the air, and slurped his wet tongue across Rachel's chin.

"Yuck! Your breath is bad!" She pushed Buddy down with her knee. "Get away from me, bad breath Buddy."

Buddy whimpered and slunk toward the barn with his tail between his legs.

Rachel hurried over to Mary, but when Mary turned to face her, she wasn't smiling. "We—we came to give you some news," she said.

Rachel looked over at her cousins, Nancy, Abe, and Sam. They weren't smiling, either. Only Uncle Ben and Aunt Irma were smiling.

"What's going on?" Rachel asked. "What news do you have?"

Mary's chin trembled, and tears gathered in her eyes. "We're gonna move away."

"Moving where?" Pap asked before Rachel could voice the question.

"To Indiana," Uncle Ben said.

Rachel looked back at Mary, and Mary gave a slow nod. "It's true."

Everyone began to talk at once.

"Why are you going to Indiana?"

"How soon do you plan to move?"

"Is your place up for sale?"

"We'll surely miss you."

Rachel stood there, too numb to say a word. Mary couldn't be moving. She had been Rachel's friend since they were little. *Oh, what will I do without Mary?* she silently moaned.

Pap held up his hand. "We can't all talk at once. Let's ask one question at a time, and then my *bruder* [brother], Ben, can answer our questions."

"Why are you moving to Indiana?" Mom asked.

"As I'm sure you all know," Uncle Ben looked at Aunt Irma, "my wife's bruder, Noah, and his family moved there last year, and Noah bought a dairy farm."

Everyone nodded.

Uncle Ben smiled. "Noah's dairy business is doing real well, and he asked me to move to Indiana and be his partner."

"But you started working at the buggy shop not long ago," Henry said. "Why would you want to quit your new job and move to Indiana?"

"I like my job at the buggy shop, but as I'm sure you know, your *daed* [dad] and I grew up on a dairy farm. I'm sure I'll enjoy working with the cows on Noah's farm even more," Uncle Ben replied.

Hearing that Mary and her family would be leaving was the worst possible news! Rachel bit off the end of her thumbnail and spit it on the ground. She'd been trying to give up her nervous habit of nail biting, but it was hard to not feel anxious about her best friend moving away. "Can't you start a dairy farm right here?" she asked.

"Our place here is too small for that," Uncle Ben said.

"Can't you buy more land?" Rachel asked.

Uncle Ben shook his head. "I'm afraid not. Land here in Lancaster County is getting too expensive, and there's not a lot of land available to buy anymore."

Rachel looked up at Aunt Irma with tears blurring her vision. "Can't Mary stay with us?"

Aunt Irma shook her head. "We could never leave any of our *kinner* [children] here. They will come to Indiana with us."

Grandpa, who stood beside Rachel, patted the top of her head. "If your folks moved somewhere else, wouldn't you want to go with them?"

Rachel looked at Mom, Pap, Jacob, Henry, and Grandpa. As much as she liked her home here, she knew if Mom and Pap decided to move, she'd want to go with them. "*Jah* [yes]," she said in a near whisper, "I'd want to move, too."

"What about Grandpa and Grandma Yoder?" Jacob asked. "Who's gonna look after them if you move away?"

Uncle Ben looked over at Pap. "As you know, our sister, Karen, and her husband, Amos, have been renting a place in Tennessee."

Pap nodded.

"Amos and Karen have decided to move to Pennsylvania and buy our house. That means they'll be living next door to our folks, same as we have been for the past twelve years."

Rachel swallowed around the lump in her throat. She didn't like the idea of someone else living in Uncle Ben and Aunt Irma's house—especially someone she didn't know very well. She'd only seen Uncle Amos and Aunt Karen a few times, and the last time she'd seen them she was seven years old. Aunt Karen had given birth to a baby boy named Gerald three years ago, but Rachel hadn't met him yet. *If only I could do something to keep Mary's family from moving,* she thought.

"When do you plan to move?" Pap asked Uncle Ben.

"Two weeks from today."

"Two weeks?" Rachel's mouth fell open.

"Why so soon?" Mom asked.

"Noah just bought fifty more cows, and now he's busier than ever," Uncle Ben replied. "He needs me there as soon as possible."

"Let us know when you're ready to start packing," Pap said. "We'll be there to help."

With tears clinging to her eyelashes, Rachel turned to Mary and gave her a hug. "I'm going to miss you so much!"

The day before Mary's family was supposed to move, Mary came over to Rachel's to spend the night.

"I can't believe this is the last time we'll ever have a

sleepover," Rachel said as the girls climbed the steps to her room.

Mary clasped Rachel's hand. "Don't say that. We'll have more sleepovers. My family will come back to Pennsylvania to visit, and your family can come see our new home in Indiana."

Rachel shook her head as tears gathered in her eyes. "It won't be the same. We won't be best friends anymore."

"We'll always be best friends," Mary said. "My moving away won't change that."

When they entered Rachel's room, Rachel flopped onto her bed with a groan. "I wish you didn't have to go. Can't you talk your folks out of moving?"

"Papa has already made up his mind." Mary set her overnight bag on the floor and joined Rachel on the bed. "Besides, the house we've lived in since before I was a baby won't be ours after Saturday. Uncle Amos and Aunt Karen are moving from Tennessee soon, and then they'll be living in our old house."

"I know." Rachel sniffed. "I just wish things could stay the same as they are right now." She touched Mary's hand. "I'm going to miss you so much, and I–I'm afraid you'll forget about me."

"Never!" Mary reached down and opened the canvas satchel she'd brought along. "I have something for you." She handed Rachel a little faceless doll with brown hair just like Mary's. "I asked my *mamm* [mom] if I could give you my doll so you would have something to remember me by."

Rachel hugged the doll close to her chest. "*Danki* [thank you], Mary. I'll think of you every time I play with this doll." She hopped off the bed and hurried across the room. "I have something to give you, too."

"What is it?"

Rachel opened the bottom drawer of her dresser and took out a rock she'd painted to look like a ladybug. "I signed my name on the bottom," she said, handing the rock to Mary. "That way you won't forget who gave it to you."

"I'll never forget you, Rachel. Thank you."

"I wish you could have brought Stripes over tonight, so he could say good-bye to Cuddles," Rachel said as she and Mary put their nightgowns on and got ready for bed.

"Mama didn't think it was a good idea," Mary said. "Stripes isn't good about staying in the yard, and if I'd brought him over to play with Cuddles, he could've run off. Since Mama and Papa are busy packing our things, they wouldn't want to be bothered with having to hunt for my cat."

"Maybe I can bring Cuddles over to your house to say good-bye," Rachel said as they crawled into bed. "I can't believe you're moving tomorrow."

Mary nodded and fluffed up her pillow.

Rachel stared at the ceiling. Even if they stayed awake all night there wouldn't be enough time to say all the things she wanted to say to Mary. Writing letters and a visit once in a while wouldn't be the same as spending the night at one another's house, playing in the haylofts in their barns, or eating lunch at school together. Tears trickled down Rachel's cheeks. After Mary moved away, nothing would ever be the same.

"Can you please open the window, Rachel?" Mary asked. "It's kind of stuffy in here."

"I suppose I could, but I have to be careful not to let Cuddles in. Mom doesn't like it when Cuddles sneaks into my room and gets up on the bed."

"We could just open it enough so some fresh air gets in."

Rachel pushed the covers aside, turned on the flashlight by her bed, and padded across the room. She'd no more than opened the window, when—*meow!*—Cuddles leaped from the tree right into her arms.

"Oh no!" Rachel exclaimed.

"Is that Cuddles?" Mary asked as she sat up in bed.

"Jah. She must have been sitting in the tree hoping I would open the window."

"Bring her over here so I can pet her."

Rachel shook her head. "No, Mary. . .Mom doesn't like me to have Cuddles on the bed. She has to go back outside."

"Don't put her out just yet. I'll come over there so I can pet Cuddles." Mary scrambled out of bed and hurried across the room.

Rachel handed the cat to Mary, and Cuddles purred loudly while Mary petted the top of her head. "She sure is soft and silky, isn't she?"

"Jah, but she'd better go back out now." Rachel opened the window wider, and was about to take the cat from Mary, when—*flap! flap!*—something flew into the room.

"What was that?" Mary squealed.

"I—I don't know. I think it might have been a bird." Rachel shined her flashlight around the room. *Woosh! Woosh!* The creature flew so fast she could barely follow it with the light.

"It's a *schpeckmaus* [bat]!" Mary dropped to the floor and dove under Rachel's bed, with Cuddles still in her arms.

Woosh! Woosh! Rachel dropped to her knees and shined the light again. Sure enough, there was a little brown bat flying around her room. "Yeow!" Rachel hollered as it swooped past her head. She ducked lower and scurried under the bed to join Mary and Cuddles.

"Wh–what are we gonna do?" Mary's voice quivered. "How are we gonna get that bat out of your room?"

"Let's lie here real quiet. Maybe it'll fly out the open window." Rachel reached over and stroked Cuddles's head for comfort.

"You don't suppose it will fly under the bed and bite us, do you?"

"I don't think so. Pap told me once that the bats we have around here aren't dangerous."

Mary giggled. "Then what are we doing under the bed?"

Rachel laughed, too. "Do you want to crawl out and see if the bat's still there?"

"No way! Do you?"

"Nope."

"Let's close our eyes and go to sleep," Mary

suggested. "When we wake up in the morning, maybe the bat will be gone."

Rachel didn't think she would sleep very comfortably on the hard floor underneath the bed, but she wasn't going to crawl out if Mary wasn't. "*Gut nacht* [good night], Mary," she said.

"Good night, Rachel."

Cock-a-doodle-do! Cock-a-doodle-do!

Rachel groaned and released a noisy yawn. The rooster was crowing; it must be morning. *Thwack!*—she bumped her head as she tried to sit up. Then she remembered—she, Mary, and Cuddles had slept under her bed to get away from the bat that flew into her room last night.

Rachel glanced over at Mary, still asleep with Cuddles in her arms. "Wake up. . .it's morning," she whispered, nudging Mary's arm.

Mary's eyes snapped open. "Is—is the bat gone?"

"I don't know. I don't hear it flying around." Rachel started to crawl out from under her bed when the bedroom door opened and Mom stepped in.

"What in the world are you doing, Rachel? And where is Mary?"

Before Rachel could respond, Mom kneeled down and peered under the bed. "What are you two doing under there, and what's Cuddles doing in your room?"

"It was stuffy in here last night," Rachel explained. "Cuddles came in when I opened the window. Then a bat flew in, and Mary and I were kind of scared, so we slept under my bed."

Mom's forehead wrinkled, and Rachel thought for sure she was in for a lecture. But then Mom's lips lifted into a smile and her eyes twinkled. "A bat got into my room once when I was a girl."

"What did you do?" asked Rachel.

"I hid under the bed." Mom held onto the bedpost and laughed so hard tears streamed down her cheeks. Rachel joined Mom's laughter, and Mary crawled out from the under the bed and started laughing, too.

Finally Mom stopped laughing. She used the corner of her apron to dry her eyes, and she looked around the room. "There's no sign of a bat in here now. It must have flown out the window."

Rachel took Cuddles from Mary. "I'll put her back in the tree."

Mom nodded. "Then we need to hurry and eat breakfast so we can take Mary home. Today's the big move, and we need to be there to help them pack."

Rachel frowned. With all the laughter going on in her room, she'd almost forgotten that Mary would be moving today.

As if she could read her thoughts, Mom patted Rachel's arm and said, "I'm glad you and Mary were able to spend the night together—even if you had to sleep under your bed."

Rachel managed a weak smile. Maybe when they got to Uncle Ben and Aunt Irma's house, she could talk them out of moving.

When Pap guided their horse and buggy onto Uncle Ben's driveway, Rachel thought she was going to break down and sob. Two big moving trucks were parked near the barn. Several people rushed around the yard, hauling boxes and furniture out of the house and into the trucks. Pap halted the horse near the hitching rail, and Mom, Mary, Grandpa, and Rachel climbed down from the buggy. Henry pulled his horse and buggy in next to Pap's, and he and Jacob climbed down from it, too.

"What can we do to help?" Pap called to Uncle Ben, who was carrying a large box out to the truck.

Uncle Ben motioned to the house with his head. "There are more boxes and furniture in there that need to be put in the trucks."

For the next few hours everyone scurried about, loading the trucks, cleaning the house, and fixing snacks for those who had come to help. By noon the house was empty and both trucks were full and ready to go.

As Rachel and Mary walked through the house together, their footsteps and voices echoed in the bare rooms. There wasn't a stick of furniture or anything else left to remind Rachel that this had been Mary and her family's home. It didn't look right to see everything gone. It wasn't right for Mary to move to Indiana.

"Mary, Nancy, Abe, and Sam. . .it's time for us to head out. Our drivers are ready to go," Uncle Ben called.

A lump formed in Rachel's throat as she looked at Mary. "I wish you didn't have to go."

"Me neither," Mary said as tears filled her eyes.

Rachel rushed over to Uncle Ben and grabbed hold of his arm. "Won't you change your mind and stay here in Pennsylvania?"

He slowly shook his head. "I'm sorry, Rachel, but our plans have been made and my bruder is expecting us to arrive at his place in a few days."

Mom hugged Aunt Irma then turned to Rachel and said, "Say good-bye to your cousins." She nodded at Jacob and Henry. "You boys need to say good-bye, too."

Mary grabbed Rachel and gave her a hug. "I'll write to you soon, I promise."

Rachel could only nod in reply. Her throat felt like it was clogged with a glob of peanut butter. No matter how much she wanted, she knew she wasn't in control of this situation. She'd learned that lesson all too well when she broke her arm a few months ago.

"We'll try to visit you soon after our *boppli* [baby] is born," Pap said as Mary's family climbed into the trucks with their drivers.

"We'll look forward to that," Aunt Irma called.

As the trucks pulled out of the driveway, Rachel thought her heart was breaking in two. She wasn't sure if she would ever see Mary again.

"You and Mary can still be friends even though you won't see each other as often as before," Mom said gently. "But you're a friendly girl, and I'm sure it won't be long until you make another best friend." She placed her hand on Rachel's slumped shoulder. "There's a little song I learned about friendship when I was a girl. Would you like me to sing it to you?"

"I guess so."

"Make new friends but keep the old," Mom sang in a clear voice. "One is silver the other is gold."

Rachel sniffed. "I—I don't want a new friend. I just want my best friend, Mary!"

Chapter 2

Verhuddelt

As Rachel walked behind Jacob on their way to school Monday morning, her heart ached. With each step she took she felt more and more depressed. Mary had moved on Saturday. Their house was empty, their barn was empty, and even Mary's desk would be empty—forever.

Rachel kicked a rock with the toe of her sneaker. "It's Uncle Ben's fault," she mumbled under her breath. "He shouldn't have taken Mary away."

Jacob nudged Rachel's arm. "*Was fehlt dir denn?* [What's the matter with you?] What are you *gemmummelt* [mumbling] about?"

"I wasn't mumbling."

"Jah, you were."

"I was just thinking about Mary moving and how much I'm going to miss her."

"They said they'd come to visit," Jacob reminded her. "And after Mom has the boppli, maybe we can make a trip to Indiana and visit them, too."

"But it could be a long time before they come back here for a visit. Mom might not feel up to traveling with the baby for a long time, either." Rachel swallowed hard, hoping she wouldn't cry in front of Jacob. If she did, he would probably call her a little *bensel* [silly child].

"I'm going to miss everyone in Mary's family, too," Jacob said, "but I won't go around all droopy because they're gone."

"I'm not droopy," Rachel said, frowning.

"*Jah*, you are."

Rachel clamped her mouth shut and hurried ahead, refusing to argue with Jacob anymore. They walked on in silence—Jacob whistling—Rachel kicking stones as she thought about how much she already missed Mary.

When they arrived at the schoolhouse, Rachel spotted Orlie down on his knees, staring at something in the grass. Curious as to what it might be, Rachel hurried over to Orlie.

"Look what I found!" he said excitedly.

"What is it?"

"It's a painted ladybug rock. It must be the one you made for my birthday in February." He grinned and held the rock out to her. "Now that it's spring and the snow's melted, it was easy to find the rock!"

"That's nice." Rachel had almost forgotten about the painted rock she'd made for Orlie's birthday and had accidentally dropped in the snow.

"You don't seem very excited about the rock. Isn't it amazing that I found it?" Orlie asked.

She only shrugged in reply.

"What's wrong? Why do you look so sad?"

The mysterious glob of peanut butter clogged Rachel's throat again and she swallowed a couple of times. "Mary and her family moved to Indiana on Saturday."

"I probably would have known that if we'd had church yesterday," Orlie said.

Rachel nodded. The Amish church they belonged to had church every other Sunday, and they took turns having it in one another's homes.

"How come Mary's family moved to Indiana?" Orlie asked.

"Her daed's going to help run a dairy farm." Rachel frowned. "It won't be the same with Mary gone."

Just then an Amish girl who looked to be about Rachel's age walked across the yard toward them. She had dark brown hair and matching eyes, and a deep dimple in each cheek. Rachel had never seen the girl before and figured she must be new. "What have you got there?" the girl asked, pointing at the rock in Orlie's hand.

Orlie smiled. "It's a ladybug rock."

She wrinkled her nose. "I don't like bugs!"

"Not even ladybugs?" Orlie asked.

She shook her head. "I don't like any kind of bugs."

Orlie looked at Rachel and said, "Have you met Audra Burkholder yet?"

Rachel shook her head.

"Audra and her family moved to the farm next to our place on Saturday." Orlie grinned. "Guess Saturday must have been moving day here in Lancaster County."

Rachel gritted her teeth. Was Orlie trying to make her feel worse about Mary moving?

"We used to live in Ohio, but we moved here to be closer to my *grossdaadi* [grandfather] and *grossmudder* [grandmother]." Audra looked at Rachel. "What's your name?"

"Rachel Yoder."

"Rachel's grandpa used to live in Ohio. Isn't that right, Rachel?" Orlie asked.

Rachel only nodded in reply. She didn't want to talk to Orlie or the new girl named Audra right now. "I think I'd better get inside," she said as she started walking toward the schoolhouse.

"What's the hurry?" Orlie called. "Elizabeth hasn't rung the bell yet."

Rachel ignored him and hurried up the schoolhouse stairs. After she put her lunch pail on the shelf just inside the door, she trudged over to her desk and sat down. She glanced at Mary's old desk and blinked back tears. For the rest of this school year Rachel would have to look at the empty desk across from her and be reminded that her best friend moved away.

A few minutes later, Elizabeth rang the school bell. *Clang! Clang! Clang!*

The children filed into the room and took their seats. Audra stood up front by the teacher's desk, red-faced and staring at the floor.

"Good morning, boys and girls," Elizabeth said.

"Good morning, Elizabeth," the scholars replied in unison.

"We have a new girl with us today. Her name is Audra Burkholder. Audra and her family moved here from Ohio." Elizabeth nudged Audra's arm. "Would you like to tell the class something about yourself?"

Audra's face turned even redder as she raised her head and looked at the class. "Well, uh—my mamm and daed are Andy and Naomi, and I have four older brothers. Walter and Perry are married. Jared's sixteen, so he's out of school already. Brian, my youngest brother, is twelve. Brian's not here today because he has a bad cold." Audra looked at the teacher. "Oh, and starting today, my daed and Jared will be working at the buggy shop."

Rachel cringed. Uncle Ben used to work at the buggy shop, until he decided he'd rather be milking cows. *I wish Uncle Ben still worked at the buggy shop, not Audra's daed and bruder.*

"We're happy to have you in our class, Audra." Elizabeth looked at the scholars and smiled. "During recess you'll have a chance to get to know Audra better. Please make her feel welcome." She pointed to Mary's empty desk. Rachel's heart skipped a beat. "That desk will be yours, Audra."

No! No! No! Rachel silently screamed. Tears burned in her eyes as she watched Audra sit at Mary's desk. Audra opened her backpack, took out a writing tablet and some books, and lifted the lid of the desk to put them inside.

When Rachel realized her mouth was hanging open, she snapped her jaw shut. *Mary's things should be in there—not Audra's,* she thought. *This isn't right. It's not right at all!*

Elizabeth picked up her Bible. "I'll be reading from Ecclesiastes 4:9–10: 'Two are better than one, because they have a good return for their work: If one falls down, his friend can help him up. But pity the man who falls and has no one to help him up!' "

Rachel's heart clenched. Mary had been that kind of friend. Whenever Rachel felt sad, Mary cheered her up. Now Rachel had no best friend, except maybe Orlie. After he'd helped Rachel with her lines in the Christmas program last year, they'd had a secret friendship. Even so, she didn't think of him as a "best friend."

Orlie's sharp whisper jolted Rachel out of her thoughts. "We're supposed to stand. It's time to repeat the Lord's Prayer."

Rachel stood and recited the prayer with the others, even though her heart wasn't in it. When she filed to the front of the room with the rest of the children to sing a few songs, her throat felt swollen. She moved to stand next to Orlie, but Audra squeezed in where Rachel wanted to stand. She sighed, slumped her shoulders, and found a spot at the end of the line.

Rachel glanced at the clock on the far wall. She would be glad when it was time for morning recess and she could go outside to play. Maybe she and Orlie could talk about the ladybug rock she'd painted for him. She might also ask if he could come over to their place and help Jacob train Buddy.

The next hour ticked by slowly as Rachel worked on her arithmetic lesson. Every few minutes she glanced at the clock. Finally, Elizabeth announced that it was time for recess.

Rachel hurried outside and was happy to see that the sun shone brightly. It had been hiding behind the clouds on the walk to school. She spotted Orlie standing near the teeter-totter. She was about to head that way when she saw Audra walk up to him. No way was she going over there now!

Rachel moved over to the swings and sat down. She let her feet dangle but didn't pump her legs. It didn't feel right to swing without Mary.

Phoebe Wagler took the other swing and started pumping her legs. *Pump, pump, swing. Pump, pump, swing.* The swing moved back and forth, and Phoebe giggled excitedly. "This is so much fun! I love to swing!"

Rachel stared at the ground.

"When's your mamm due to have her boppli, Rachel?" Phoebe asked.

"This summer—probably July." Rachel decided to get her swing moving, too. Maybe then Phoebe would stop talking to her. *Pump, pump, swing. Pump, pump, swing.*

"My baby sister, Darlene, is ten weeks old." Phoebe grinned. "It's so cute when she gurgles and coos. I don't think there's anything sweeter than a boppli."

Rachel hoped her baby sister or brother would be cute and sweet. She didn't like the idea of having a fussy baby in the house.

The bell rang, calling everyone back inside. Rachel left the swing and hurried into the schoolhouse. She'd just taken her seat when Orlie turned in his chair and said, "Audra told me her daed might let her visit the buggy shop on Saturday. She invited me to go along. How about you, Rachel? Would you like to see the buggy shop, too?"

Rachel shook her head. "I've seen it already—when my uncle Ben worked there."

"Oh." Orlie turned around before Rachel could say anything more. So much for asking if Orlie might come over to their place on Saturday. He obviously had other plans.

At eleven thirty, Elizabeth dismissed the classroom by rows to get their lunch pails. Rachel frowned when Audra's row was dismissed first.

When Rachel reached up to take her lunch pail down from the shelf, Jacob took his down at the same time. "Are you in a better mood now, Rachel?" he asked.

She narrowed her eyes at him. "What do you think?"

"I think you're an old sourpuss today. If Mom packed a bottle of Pap's homemade root beer in your lunch pail, maybe you'll be sweeter after you drink it."

"It would take more than a bottle of root beer to make *you* sweeter," Rachel muttered as she headed out to the porch to eat her lunch. She took a seat on the top step, opened her lunch pail, and took out her sandwich. Her stomach rumbled as she removed the plastic wrapping. Peanut butter and jelly was her favorite kind. She lifted it to her mouth and was about to take a bite, when a fishy smell wafted up to her nose.

"Eww. . .tuna!"

But how could that be? Rachel wondered. She'd watched Mom make her sandwich this morning, and it had been peanut butter and jelly—not tuna fish!

She looked in the lunch pail and saw an orange, two cookies, and a bottle of milk. *This isn't the lunch Mom made for me!*

Rachel looked across the porch, where several other girls sat, and spotted Audra—eating a peanut butter and jelly sandwich!

Rachel tossed the tuna sandwich in the lunch pail and slammed the lid. Then she marched over to Audra and said, "I believe that's my sandwich you're eating!"

Audra looked up at Rachel and wrinkled her forehead. "What makes you think that?"

Rachel handed the lunch pail to Audra. "There's a tuna fish sandwich in here, and it's not mine. You're eating *my* peanut butter and jelly sandwich." She pointed to the lunch pail sitting on the porch beside Audra. "And that's *my* lunch pail!"

Audra's eyes widened as she looked at one lunch pail and then the other. "I think I made a mistake," she said. "Our lunch pails look almost alike. They must have gotten verhuddelt. Since I've already eaten part of your sandwich, why don't you go ahead and eat my lunch?"

Rachel shook her head so hard the ties on her *kapp* [cap] flipped around her face. "No way! I hate the taste of tuna!"

Audra shrugged and handed the half-eaten peanut butter and jelly sandwich to Rachel. "All right then. Here you go."

Rachel nearly gagged. "No thanks!" She wasn't about to eat that peanut butter and jelly sandwich now. Not with Audra's germs on it! "I'll bet you took my lunch pail on purpose!"

Audra shook her head. "Why would I do that? I didn't know the lunch pail I took was yours. I thought it was mine."

Rachel bent down, snatched her lunch pail, and shoved Audra's lunch pail in its place. At least she could eat the apple and banana bread Mom had packed.

She plopped down on her seat across the porch step and opened the lid. Sure enough, there was a big red apple and two slices of banana bread.

Rachel unwrapped the banana bread and was about to take a bite when she remembered that Mary liked banana bread, too. Rachel's eyes filled with tears. She tossed the banana bread into the lunch pail and shut the lid with a *snap!* She wasn't hungry anymore.

"Aren't you gonna eat your banana bread?" Jacob asked, taking a seat beside Rachel.

She shook her head. "I can't."

"Why not?"

"It reminds me of Mary."

The skin around Jacob's blue eyes wrinkled. "Huh?"

"Banana bread was one of Mary's favorites." Rachel sighed. "Now that Mary's gone, every time I see a piece of banana bread, I'll think of her."

"That's *lecherich* [ridiculous], Rachel." Jacob grabbed her lunch pail, flipped open the lid, and helped himself to the pieces of banana bread.

"Hey!" Rachel frowned at him. "What do you think you're doing?"

He shrugged. "Figured if you're not gonna eat the banana bread then I will."

Rachel was about to say something mean to Jacob when she noticed several children staring at her. "Fine then, I hope you enjoy every bite!" She jumped up, raced down the steps, and ran all the way to the swings.

As Rachel walked home from school that afternoon, she kept thinking about the lunch pail mix up and how happy Audra had looked eating Rachel's peanut butter and jelly sandwich. "I'll do something to make sure that doesn't happen again," Rachel muttered under her breath.

Jacob nudged Rachel's arm. "You're mumbling again, just like you did this morning. What's wrong now?"

As they continued walking, Rachel told Jacob about Audra eating her peanut butter and jelly sandwich. "I think she took my lunch pail on purpose because she doesn't like me," she grumbled.

"Audra's new at our school," Jacob said. "She doesn't know you well enough to decide whether she likes you or not."

"Humph!" Rachel grunted. "I could tell by the way she looked at me that she doesn't like me."

"You're lecherich, little bensel." Jacob shook his head and kept walking.

"I'm not ridiculous, and I wish you would stop calling me a silly child!"

"When you stop acting like a silly child, I'll stop calling you one."

As Rachel hurried on, an idea popped into her head. *When I get home, I'm going to paint a picture of a ladybug on my lunch pail. That should keep Audra from thinking it's hers!*

When Rachel and Jacob arrived home, Jacob went out to the dog run to see Buddy, and Rachel hurried to the house. She set her lunch pail on the kitchen counter and went upstairs to her room to get out her paints. When she returned to the kitchen, she spread some newspaper on the table, placed her lunch pail on it, and opened a bottle of black paint. She had just finished painting the body of the ladybug on one side of her lunch pail when Mom entered the kitchen.

"What are you doing, Rachel?"

"I'm painting a ladybug on both sides of my lunch pail."

Mom squinted over the top of her metal-framed glasses. "Why would you want to do something like that?"

"Because there's a new girl at school named Audra

Burkholder, and our lunch pails got verhuddelt because
she took mine instead of hers. The sandwich in the
lunch pail I opened was tuna fish—not peanut butter
and jelly." Rachel frowned. "I think Audra took my
lunch on purpose."

"Do your lunch pails look alike?" Mom asked.

"Jah."

"Then I'm sure Audra took your lunch pail by
mistake."

Rachel stared at her lunch pail and heaved a big sigh.
"Elizabeth gave Mary's old desk to Audra, and now
every time I look over there I'll be reminded that Mary's
gone and I lost my best friend."

Mom clucked her tongue. "I don't think you're being
fair, Rachel. Audra's new at your school, and I'm sure she
needs a friend. You should give her a chance, don't you
think?"

Rachel shrugged.

"Why don't you invite Audra over to play after
school? You might become good friends."

"I don't need a friend. Not a friend like Audra,
anyway." Rachel thought about Sherry, the English
girl she'd met at the farmer's market last summer, and
wondered if she would make a good friend. Sherry had
let Rachel walk her dog, even though they'd just met.
The only problem was, Rachel didn't know where Sherry
lived, and she hadn't seen her since that day at the
market. Rachel needed a friend now. She needed Mary!

Mom moved over to the cupboard and took out a

glass. "Sometimes the very thing we think we don't want is exactly what we need," she said as she filled her glass with water.

I don't need Audra, Rachel thought. *And I don't want her, either.* Rachel dipped a clean brush into the jar of white paint so she could paint the ladybug's eyes and antennas. She was sure of one thing—she could never be Audra Burkholder's friend!

Chapter 3

Raining Sideways

It's raining pretty hard. You'd better wear your boots to school this morning," Mom said as she handed Rachel her lunch pail with a ladybug painted on both sides.

Rachel peeked out the kitchen window and wrinkled her nose. Not a speck of sun. "I hate the rain!"

Mom looked at Rachel over the top of her glasses. "You know how I feel about that word *hate*."

"I know, but I just don't like walking to school in the rain." Rachel set the lunch pail on the floor, slipped her feet into her rubber boots, and put on her raincoat. "If it keeps raining, we probably won't get to play outside during recess today."

"It's been a dry spring so far and we need a good soaking," Mom said. "If you can't play outside during recess, I'm sure you'll find something fun to do indoors."

"Maybe you can sit at your desk and draw a picture, little bensel," Jacob said as he joined Rachel in the utility room.

"Stop calling your sister that name," Mom said before Rachel could respond. "She is not a silly child."

Rachel smiled to herself. At least she wasn't the only one being scolded by Mom this morning.

"We'd better get going or we're gonna be late for school," Jacob said, nudging Rachel's arm.

"Just let me get my umbrella." Rachel opened the closet door, but her umbrella wasn't there. "Has anyone seen my umbrella?"

"Where did you put it?" Mom asked.

"I thought it was in here." Rachel squinted at Jacob. "Did you take my umbrella?"

He grunted. "Why would I want your *dumm* [dumb] old umbrella?"

"It's not dumb and it's not old," Rachel said. "Esther gave it to me for Christmas." Rachel's older sister always gave Rachel nice presents for her birthday and Christmas, and Rachel would feel bad if she lost the umbrella.

Jacob opened the back door. "Let's go, Rachel."

"I'm not going without my umbrella."

"Aw, come on. You won't melt from a little bit of rain." Jacob snickered and shook his head.

Rachel looked out the door. "That's more than a little rain. It's coming down by the buckets. The drainage ditch out by the road is so full, it's starting to overflow. If the rain doesn't stop soon, Pap's fields will flood and turn into ponds."

"I can't believe the way you exaggerate." Jacob

stepped onto the porch. "Are you coming or not?"

Rachel frowned. "It's raining too hard to walk without an umbrella."

Mom went to the kitchen and returned with a large black umbrella. "You may borrow my umbrella today," she said, handing it to Rachel.

"Danki, Mom." Rachel picked up her lunch pail and slipped it into her backpack.

Mom bent down and gave Rachel a hug. Then she patted Jacob's shoulder. "Have a good day."

"You, too, Mom," Rachel and Jacob said at the same time.

Rachel opened the umbrella and sloshed down the muddy driveway behind Jacob. When they reached the edge of the road she noticed there were puddles everywhere.

Rachel walked carefully, stepping around the puddles. Any other time she would have enjoyed plodding through the puddles, but not today. She dreaded going to school—dreaded seeing Audra sitting at Mary's desk—dreaded having to stay indoors for recess.

Woosh! The wind picked up and whipped against Rachel's legs, making it hard for her to walk. *Splat! Splat! Splat!* The rain splattered on her umbrella and splashed against the part of her dress that hung below her raincoat.

"Hurry up, slowpoke," Jacob called over his shoulder. "You're walking too slow."

"I can't walk any faster because it's raining sideways

and the wind's slowing me down," Rachel complained. Her day was off to a very bad start.

"It's not raining sideways. The wind's just blowing the rain, that's all. What a bensel you are."

"Mom said you're not supposed to call me a silly child anymore."

Jacob grunted and kept walking.

Rachel gripped the umbrella tighter. Deep down she sometimes wished she could do something so Jacob would get in trouble.

Woosh! Another gust of wind came up, and—*floop!*—Rachel's umbrella turned inside out. "No, no, no," she groaned. "Always trouble somewhere!"

Struggling against the blustery wind and drenching rain, Rachel tried to pull the umbrella right side out. It didn't budge. The wind was too strong, and the rain poured down so hard she could barely see.

"Would it help if I walked slower and closer to you so I can block the wind?" Jacob asked.

Rachel wasn't sure why Jacob was being so nice all of a sudden, but she really didn't think him walking closer to her would help that much. "Danki anyway," she said, "but you'd better keep moving. If we walk any slower we'll be late to school."

Jacob shrugged and continued on. Rachel trudged wearily behind.

By the time they arrived at the schoolhouse Rachel was wet and cold. As she stepped onto the porch, she looked up at the sky and spotted a ray of sun peeking through the clouds. She hoped this was the end of her troubles for today.

Elizabeth rang the bell, and Rachel followed Jacob inside. She'd just slipped out of her raincoat and boots when Orlie walked up and pointed at her umbrella. "What happened to that?" he asked with a snicker.

"It turned inside out because of the wind."

"It sure looks funny." He laughed some more. "I'll bet you had a hard time staying dry under that, huh?"

"Very funny!" Rachel struggled with the umbrella but finally got it turned right side out again. Next she took her lunch pail out of her backpack and was about to place it on the shelf near the door when Phoebe tapped her on the shoulder. "Did you get a new lunch pail? I like those cute little ladybugs."

"This is my old lunch pail. I painted lady bugs on both sides so no one would think the lunch pail was hers." Rachel glanced over at Audra, who sat on the floor struggling to take off her boots.

Audra wrinkled her nose and turned her back to Rachel.

"I wish I had a ladybug painted on my lunch pail," Phoebe said. "You're really good at art, Rachel."

Rachel felt pleased knowing someone thought she could paint well. "Would you like me to paint something on your lunch pail?" she asked Phoebe.

"Oh, jah. Could you do a ladybug like yours?"

Rachel shook her head. "If I put a ladybug on your lunch pail, then it will look like my lunch pail and we might get them verhuddelt."

"How about a butterfly or a turtle?" Phoebe suggested. "Could you paint one of those?"

"Jah, sure, if it's all right with your mamm." Phoebe was two years younger than Rachel, and Rachel didn't think it would be right to paint anything on Phoebe's lunch pail unless Phoebe's mother gave her permission.

"I'll ask Mama when I get home." Phoebe smiled. "Can you bring your paints to school tomorrow?"

Rachel nodded. "If your mamm says it okay, maybe I can paint something on your lunch pail during our lunch recess."

"That'd be good." Phoebe scurried off to her desk, and Rachel did the same. Maybe this wouldn't be such a bad day after all.

Elizabeth opened her Bible and had just started reading from Matthew 5:22, when Aaron King, the boy who sat behind Rachel, tapped her on the shoulder. "*Psst. . .*Rachel. . .I heard about the ladybugs you painted on your lunch pail," he whispered.

Rachel only nodded in reply. She knew everyone was expected to be quiet during the time of scripture reading.

Aaron tapped her shoulder again. "I also heard you're gonna bring your paints to school tomorrow. Could you paint a frog on my lunch pail?"

Rachel smiled. It was nice to know someone else appreciated her artwork.

"*Psst. . .*Rachel, did you hear what I said?"

Rachel turned around. "Jah, Aaron," she said,

forgetting to whisper. "If your folks don't mind, I'd be happy to paint something on your lunch pail."

"Rachel Yoder, stop talking and turn around. You know better than to do that when I'm reading from the Bible."

Rachel jumped at the sound of her teacher's voice. Her face heated up as she turned toward the front of the room. She raised her hand.

"What is it, Rachel?"

"Aaron was asking if I could—"

Elizabeth shook her head. "You're the one who was turned around, and your voice was the only one I heard. Make sure it doesn't happen again."

Rachel's face grew hotter. *It's Aaron's fault I got in trouble. He should be in trouble with Elizabeth, too.* She tried to concentrate on the verse of scripture Elizabeth was reading about not being angry with others, but all she could think about was how the teacher had embarrassed her in front of the class and how Aaron had gotten her in trouble. She squeezed her eyes shut to keep tears from falling. *I'm not going to paint anything on Aaron's lunch pail now!*

When the scripture, prayer, and songs were done, it was time for arithmetic. Rachel had just opened her math book, when—*bzzz. . .bzzz*—a pesky fly flew past her nose. *Bzzz. . .bzzz. . .bzzz.*

Rachel swatted at the fly, but it buzzed past her again. Maybe, if she was real fast, she could catch that irritating fly in her hand. It couldn't be that hard; she'd seen her brother Henry do it many times.

Rachel kept a close watch on the fly as it zipped over Orlie's head, flew around Audra's desk, and zoomed back to her own desk.

When the fly buzzed in front of Rachel's face, she reached out, and—*woosh!*—trapped the fly in her hand.

R-r-zzz. . .r-r-zzz. . . Rachel felt the vibration of the fly's wings flapping against her fingers and palm.

With a satisfied smile, Rachel held her hand up to her ear. *R-r-zzz. . .r-r-zzz. . .* She heard the fly buzzing.

Elizabeth left her desk and headed down the center aisle. "What have you got in your hand?" she asked, stopping in front of Rachel's desk.

Everyone in the room stopped what they were doing and turned to look at Rachel. Rachel's face heated up. "There's—uh—a fly in my hand."

Elizabeth's forehead wrinkled. "A fly?"

Rachel nodded.

"What are you doing with a fly in your hand?"

"It was bothering me, so I caught it."

"Well, please let it go and finish your arithmetic lesson."

Rachel opened her hand, and—*zip!*—the fly flew straight up and landed on Elizabeth's nose. The children all laughed, but Elizabeth frowned. She swatted at the fly as it buzzed across the room. Then it circled Sharon Smucker, the teacher's helper, darted over Aaron's head, and flew toward Rachel's desk. Rachel reached out, and—*woosh!*—the fly was trapped in her hand again.

Elizabeth's mouth dropped open, and the children all clapped.

Rachel smiled. "Would you like me to put the fly outside?"

Elizabeth nodded. "Please do. And be sure to wash your hands once you've let the fly go."

Rachel headed to the back of the room, opened the door, and released the pesky fly. Then she hurried to the outdoor pump, washed her hands, and raced back inside.

When she returned to her seat, Elizabeth told the class to turn in their papers. "It's not raining anymore and the sun is beginning to shine, so you may go outside for recess," she said.

Rachel didn't bother to put on her coat or boots before hurrying out the door.

"That was sure something the way you caught that fly in your hand," Orlie said when he caught up to Rachel near the swings. "How'd you learn to do that anyway?"

She smiled, noticing that Orlie didn't smell like garlic today. Maybe his mother had quit making him eat a piece of garlic every day like she'd done last winter. "I learned to catch flies by watching my brother Henry," she said. "He does it all the time."

"Do you think you can teach me how to catch a fly?" Orlie asked.

"I suppose I could."

"*Eww. . .*I'd never want to touch a dirty old fly. I don't like bugs at all," Audra said, stepping between

Rachel and Orlie. She looked at Rachel and wrinkled her nose. "How could you stand touching that filthy fly? Aren't you worried about getting germs?"

"My little sister's not worried about that at all," Jacob said before Rachel could respond. "She's already got the fly flu."

Audra's eyes widened. "The fly flu?"

Jacob nodded. "That's right."

"How did you get the fly flu?" Audra asked Rachel.

Rachel was about to tell Audra that she'd better stay away from her, because the fly flu was contagious, when Orlie said, "There's no such thing as the fly flu. Rachel's bruder just likes to tease."

Jacob snorted a laugh and slapped his knee. "Once, when Rachel made a shoofly pie, it turned out so bad we all thought we were gonna come down with the fly flu."

Rachel poked Jacob's arm. "If you don't stop saying mean things, when we get home I'll tell Mom you were teasing me again."

"You do and I'll tell Mom that you were showing off in class today."

"I was not."

"Were so."

"Was not."

"I don't know about you, Orlie," Audra spoke up, "but I'm not going to stay here and listen to these two argue."

"Me neither," said Orlie. "Let's head over to the swings."

As Audra tromped past Rachel, she stepped in a mud

puddle, and—*splat!*—a wave of mud splashed up and all over Rachel's new dress!

Rachel groaned. "What'd you do that for, Audra?"

Audra's face turned red. "I–I'm sorry."

Rachel looked down at her dress and clenched her fists. "My mamm's not going to be happy when she sees that I've got mud all over my new dress."

"I didn't do it on purpose," Audra said. "It was just an accident."

Rachel whirled around and headed back to the schoolhouse. *I don't care what Audra says. I'll bet she stepped in that mud puddle on purpose because she doesn't like me. Well, I don't like her, either.*

As Rachel and Jacob walked home from school that afternoon, it started to rain.

"Oh, great," Rachel complained. "I hope it doesn't rain sideways again."

Jacob ignored her and kept walking.

Rachel looked down at her dirty dress. "I'm mad at Audra for splattering mud all over my dress," she grumbled. "I'm sure she did it on purpose, too."

Jacob shook his head. "I doubt it, Rachel."

"Humph! A lot you know."

"I heard Audra and Orlie talking during recess, and Audra seemed nice enough to me. Maybe you need to give her a chance."

"I wouldn't be surprised if Mom makes me wash my dress, the way she did last summer when I fell in the pond during our end-of-the-school-year picnic," Rachel said, ignoring Jacob's comment about Audra.

Jacob halted and turned to face Rachel. "If you're so upset about the mud, why don't you hold out your skirt and the let rain wash it off?"

Rachel grunted. "That's a crazy idea, Jacob."

"No it's not. Just hold out the side of your skirt and let the rain wash it clean."

"But then my dress will be sopping wet."

"Would you rather that it be wet or dirty?"

"Neither."

"Then quit complaining."

"I'm not."

"Jah, you are. You've had a bad attitude ever since Mary moved away."

Rachel swallowed around the lump in her throat. She didn't need Jacob to remind her of how miserable she felt without Mary. And she didn't like him sticking up for Audra. Rain splattered Rachel's cheeks, mixing with her tears. She felt like she'd been rained on all day.

By the time Rachel's house came into view, her legs were so wet they felt like two limp noodles. She trudged up the back steps behind Jacob and followed him into the house.

Rachel's teeth chattered as she slipped out of her raincoat and boots. She opened Mom's umbrella and set it on the floor in the corner of the utility room so it could dry.

"Mmm. . .I smell something good." Jacob's nose

twitched as he hung his coat on a wall peg near the door. "I'll bet Mom made a batch of cookies today."

The sweet smell of cinnamon and molasses drew Rachel into the kitchen where she saw Mom removing a tray of cookies from the oven.

"I knew it. . .cookies!" Jacob smacked his lips.

"Oh, Rachel, I found your umbrella after you left for school this morning. It was under your bed." Mom turned with a smile on her face, but when she looked at Rachel, her smile disappeared. "*Ach* [oh], Rachel, what happened to your dress?"

"That new girl, Audra, stepped in a puddle during recess and splattered mud all over me," Rachel said. "I think she did it on purpose because she doesn't like me."

"What makes you so sure she doesn't like you?" Mom asked.

"I think it's Rachel who doesn't like Audra," Jacob said before Rachel could reply. "She's still mad at Audra for eating her peanut butter sandwich yesterday."

Mom looked at Rachel over the top of her glasses. "Is that so, Rachel?"

Rachel nodded. "Audra didn't take my lunch pail today, though. Everyone knew it was mine since I painted ladybugs on both sides of it. In fact, two of the kinner asked if I'd paint something on their lunch pails."

"You paint very well, so I'm sure you'll do a nice job."

"Is it all right if I take my paints and brushes tomorrow so I can paint something on Phoebe's and Aaron's lunch pails?" Rachel asked.

51

"I suppose it would be all right." Mom pointed to Rachel's dress. "In the meantime, run upstairs and get changed out of that dress. When you come back down I'll have some cookies and hot chocolate waiting."

"Danki, Mom." Rachel hurried up the stairs, smiling to herself. Mom hadn't seemed that upset about the mud-splattered dress. Maybe she wouldn't make Rachel wash it after all.

When Rachel returned to the kitchen, she took a seat at the table across from Jacob. Mom placed a plate of ginger cookies in the middle of the table and gave Rachel and Jacob mugs of hot chocolate. "Would either of you like some marshmallows to go in your hot chocolate?"

Jacob nodded eagerly and so did Rachel. Mom took a bag of marshmallows from the cupboard and handed it to Jacob. He took three, gave the bag to Rachel, and she took four. She popped one in her mouth and dropped the other three in her mug.

Mom poured herself a cup of hot chocolate and took a seat beside Rachel. "Did you put your dirty dress in the laundry basket?"

Rachel nodded. "I put my wet stockings in there, too."

"I'll wash clothes tomorrow." Mom glanced at the raindrops splattered against the kitchen window. "If it continues to rain, I'll have to hang the clean clothes in the cellar."

"I hope Buddy stayed dry in his doghouse today," Jacob said. "When I'm done with my hot chocolate I think I'll go outside and check on him."

"I'm going out to the barn to see Cuddles," Rachel said. "After that, I may write Mary a letter."

"Speaking of Mary. . ." Mom smiled at Rachel. "When I checked the answering machine in our phone shed this morning, there was a message from your aunt Irma."

Rachel's eyes widened. "What'd she say?"

"Just that they'd made it to Indiana and will call again or write a letter after they get settled in."

"Was there a message for me from Mary?"

Mom shook her head. "I'm afraid not, but I'm sure Mary will write to you soon."

A lump formed in Rachel's throat and she swallowed hard. If Mary hadn't cared enough to give her mamm a message for Rachel then maybe Rachel wouldn't bother to write Mary a letter after all.

"I—I think I'll go out to the barn and see Cuddles," she mumbled.

"Mom pointed to Rachel's mug. "You haven't finished drinking your hot chocolate yet."

"I'll finish it when I come back inside."

Jacob rolled his eyes. "It'll be cold by then, little bensel."

"Jacob Yoder, what have I told you about calling your sister a silly child?" Mom squinted at Jacob over the top of her glasses.

"Sorry," he mumbled.

Mom patted Rachel's hand. "Go on out to the barn.

When you come back to the house I'll heat your hot chocolate for you."

"Danki." Rachel pushed away from the table, grabbed her raincoat, and rushed out the door.

"Cuddles. . .where are you Cuddles?" Rachel panted as she raced into the barn.

"Rachel, is that you?"

Rachel glanced around. That was Grandpa's voice, but she saw no sign of him.

"Where are you, Grandpa?"

"I—I'm over here behind the hay."

Rachel hurried over to the bales of hay piled in one corner of the barn and found Grandpa down on his knees. "What's wrong, Grandpa? How come your face is all red, and why are you on your knees?"

"I was moving some bales, and I pulled a muscle in my back. It hurts something awful, and I don't think I can't get up on my own." He moaned. "Can you get me some help?"

"Jah, Grandpa. I'll be right back." Rachel dashed out of the barn and hurried into the house. She found Mom and Jacob still in the kitchen.

"Grandpa's in the barn and he hurt his back. He says he can't get up, so he sent me to get help."

Mom jumped up from her chair. "Jacob, your daed and Henry are fixing some fences on the other side of the pasture. Run out there and get them right away!"

Jacob grabbed his jacket and rushed out the door.

"I'm going out to the barn to be with my daed,"

Mom said to Rachel. "You can either wait here or come along."

"I'll come with you." Rachel followed Mom out the door, praying that Grandpa would be okay.

Chapter 4
Unexpected Company

Rachel did what she could to help Grandpa Schrock feel better, like playing games with him and bringing him water and special treats like Mom's ginger cookies while he rested in bed. The doctor said Grandpa pulled a muscle in his lower back and gave Grandpa some medicine for the pain. The doctor also told Grandpa to rest his back until the swelling went down. So every day after school, Rachel sat next to Grandpa's bed and listened as he told her about the greenhouse he wanted to build in the spring. He hadn't told Pap about the idea yet, and said he figured until his back got better, there was no point in mentioning it. Right now the best thing he could do was rest.

Helping Mom take care of Grandpa made Rachel feel a little less lonely for Mary, and things were somewhat better at school now, too. Rachel took her paints to school the day after she'd taken her ladybug lunch pail. She painted a turtle on Aaron's lunch pail and a butterfly on Phoebe's lunch pail. When the others saw what a good job she could do, several asked her to paint their lunch pails, too.

On Saturday, Rachel decided she would spend the morning visiting with Grandpa.

Tap. . .tap. . .tap. She knocked on his bedroom door. No answer.

"Grandpa, are you awake?"

Still no answer.

Rachel pressed her ear against the door. *Zzzzzz. . .* Soft snoring sounds came from Grandpa's room. He was obviously taking a nap.

Rachel headed to the kitchen, where Mom was busy making a shoofly pie. At least she hadn't asked Rachel to help make it. The last time Rachel had made a shoofly pie she left out the sugar and put in too much salt. It tasted awful, and Jacob made sure Rachel knew about it.

"Is it all right if I go over to Grandma and Grandpa Yoder's house?" Rachel asked Mom. "I haven't visited with them in a while."

Mom nodded as she rolled out the pie dough. "I'm sure they would like that. Why don't you take some of the ginger cookies I made the other day? Those are Grandpa Yoder's favorite kind of cookies, you know."

"I'd be happy to take some cookies along." Rachel smiled. She knew Grandpa Yoder liked to dunk them in milk just like she did.

A short time later, Rachel headed across the field toward her grandparents' house, carrying a paper sack

full of ginger cookies. She'd thought about bringing
Cuddles along, but since Mary's cat, Stripes, wasn't there
for Cuddles to play with, she decided it would be best to
leave Cuddles at home.

Rachel hadn't been over to Grandma and Grandpa
Yoder's place since Mary and her family moved away.
Aunt Karen, Uncle Amos, and their little boy, Gerald,
lived next door to Grandma and Grandpa Yoder now.
Rachel had avoided going over there. She didn't want
to be reminded that Mary lived in Indiana now, where
Rachel would probably never get to go. It was hard not
to be angry with Uncle Ben for taking Mary away. It was
hard not to be upset with Mary for not writing Rachel
any letters. Of course, Rachel hadn't written to Mary yet,
either. She'd been waiting for Mary to write to her first.

Maybe I'll write Mary a letter when I get home today,
Rachel decided as her grandparents' house came into
view. *Then I can tell her about Grandpa Schrock's sore back
and my visit with Grandma and Grandpa Yoder.* Since
Mary and her family had lived next door to Grandma
and Grandpa Yoder for several years, Mary would
probably want to know how they were doing.

Rachel stepped onto Grandma and Grandpa's back
porch and knocked on the door. *Tap. . .tap. . .tap.* When
no one answered, she knocked again.

Still no answer. Maybe they'd gone next door to
Aunt Karen's.

Rachel frowned. She didn't want to go over there, but
she didn't want to miss the chance of seeing Grandma
and Grandpa, either.

With a sense of dread, she stepped onto the porch of Mary's old house and knocked on the door. *Tap. . .tap. . .* The door opened after the second knock.

"Rachel, what a surprise! We weren't expecting any visitors today," Aunt Karen said with a friendly smile.

"I came to see Grandma and Grandpa, but they didn't answer my knock. Are they here?"

Aunt Karen shook her head. "They're not home. Grandpa took Grandma to town to do some shopping today. I don't expect they'll be home until late this afternoon."

Struggling with the urge to nibble on a fingernail, Rachel fidgeted with the ties on her kapp. "Oh, I see. Guess I'll head back home then."

Rachel turned and started for the stairs, but Aunt Karen called out to her. "Won't you come in and visit? I'm sure Gerald would love to see you."

Before Rachel could reply, Gerald stuck his head out the door. When he saw Rachel, his face broke into a wide smile. "*Kumme* [come]," he said, reaching his hand out to her.

Rachel couldn't say no to the cute little blond-haired boy with eyes as blue as a summer sky. She glanced at the sack of cookies in her hand and knew it wouldn't be right if she didn't share a few with her little cousin. "Jah, okay. I'll come inside, but only for a little while."

Rachel looked at Aunt Karen and lifted the sack. "I brought some ginger cookies for Grandma and Grandpa Yoder. Maybe you and Gerald would like a few, too."

Aunt Karen smiled. "That's very nice of you, Rachel." She opened the door wider. "Let's go to the kitchen and I'll pour us some milk to go with the cookies."

"We'll need to save some for Grandma and Grandpa, though," Rachel added quickly as she followed Aunt Karen to the kitchen. "Ginger cookies are Grandpa's favorite kind."

"Of course," Aunt Karen said with a nod. "When they get home I'll see that they get the cookies."

Gerald reached up and grabbed Rachel's hand. "Kumme." He pointed to the sack. *"Kichlin* [cookies]." Then he pointed to the refrigerator. *"Millich* [milk]."

"All right, let's have some cookies." Rachel let Gerald lead her to the table. Once they were seated, she opened the sack and placed two cookies on a napkin in front of him. She gave Aunt Karen two cookies, and helped herself to two as well.

Aunt Karen poured three glasses of milk and set them on the table. Then she took a seat in the chair next to Rachel.

Rachel glanced around the room and noticed the way Aunt Karen had placed all her things. Even the battery-operated clock on the wall that made bird sounds every half hour made the kitchen look different. It was strange how much a house could change by having different people living in it. *At least there aren't strangers living in Mary's old house,* Rachel thought.

"You'll have to come back soon and bring your mamm along," Aunt Karen said.

Rachel nodded. "When she's not busy or taking a nap."

"Your mamm's expecting a boppli soon, isn't she?"

"Jah. It's supposed to be born sometime in July," Rachel said as she dunked a cookie in her glass of milk.

"I imagine you're looking forward to being a big sister."

Rachel only shrugged in reply.

"Are you hoping the baby will be a boy or a girl?" Aunt Karen asked.

"I guess it would be nice to have a little sister," Rachel said.

Aunt Karen smiled. "I'm hoping the next boppli we have will be a boy so Gerald will have a brother."

Rachel glanced over at Gerald. There was a dribble of milk running down his chin, and the floor underneath him was littered with cookie crumbs.

I suppose that's what I have to look forward to after our boppli's born and is old enough to eat by herself, Rachel thought. *I just hope I'm not expected to clean up the mess.*

When they were finished eating, Gerald hopped off his chair, grabbed Rachel's hand and said, "Gerald *schpiele gern* [like to play]."

"I'll be the *gaul* [horse] and you can be the *reider* [rider]." Rachel spoke to her cousin in Pennsylvania Dutch. Gerald only knew a few words in English and wouldn't learn to speak it well until he attended school in the first grade.

The toddler nodded enthusiastically, and Rachel

squatted down so he could climb on her back. As she crawled around the kitchen on her hands and knees, Gerald hollered, "*Fege* [run about], gaul!"

"*Kanscht seller gaul reide* [Are you able to ride that horse], Gerald?" Aunt Karen asked with a chuckle. "She looks pretty *mudich* [spirited] to me."

Gerald thumped Rachel's side with his knee and kept hollering, "Fege, gaul!"

Rachel was getting tired, and her knees started to hurt. She turned her head and was about to tell Gerald he had to get off when, *whack!*—his fist came up and punched her right in the eye!

"Ach, my eye!" Rachel cried as she pushed Gerald off and clambered to her feet.

Aunt Karen rushed forward. "Rachel, are you all right?"

Rachel blinked against stinging tears. "My eye hurts!"

"Let me take a look." Aunt Karen's forehead wrinkled. "It's watering quite a bit, and the skin around your eye is starting to swell. You'd better take a seat at the table and let me put some ice on it."

Rachel sat down, and Aunt Karen scurried over to the refrigerator.

Gerald plodded over to Rachel and reached out his hand. "Fege, gaul?"

She pushed his hand aside. "Go away. It's your fault my eye's sore and swollen."

"I'm sure Gerald didn't do it on purpose," Aunt Karen said as she handed Rachel a small bag of ice.

"Gerald, tell Cousin Rachel you're sorry."

"*Es dutt mir leed* [I am sorry]," he said.

Rachel held the ice against her eye as she clamped her lips together. She didn't think Gerald was one bit sorry. He'd only said he was sorry because Aunt Karen had told him to.

Gerald grunted then he let lose with a loud, *"Wa-a-a!"* Rachel ignored him.

Aunt Karen peeked under the ice bag. "It looks like your eye is going to be okay, Rachel, and Gerald really wants you to forgive him."

Rachel knew what she had to do. Even though in her heart she hadn't forgiven Gerald, she nodded and said, "I forgive you."

By the time Rachel returned home, her eye felt pretty much back to normal. As she rounded the corner of the house, she was surprised to see a horse and buggy tied to their hitching rail. Had Mom gotten some unexpected company?

Rachel hurried into the house. When she stepped into the kitchen, she halted, horrified at what she saw. Audra's mother, Naomi, sat at the table drinking a cup of tea, and Audra sat on the floor holding Cuddles!

Mom turned to Rachel and smiled. "Audra and her mamm stopped by for a visit."

Rachel was frozen in shock. She just stood there staring at Cuddles, who purred loudly as Audra stroked her ear. *Traitor!* she thought. *How could you cozy up to someone who doesn't even like me?*

"Audra's brother, Brian, is upstairs with Jacob. Rachel, why don't you take Audra up to your room so you can play and get better acquainted?" Mom suggested.

Playing with Audra was the last thing Rachel wanted to do, but she knew better than to argue with Mom—especially in front of guests.

Rachel looked at Audra and fought the urge to bite a fingernail. "*Duh die katz naus* [put the cat out]. Mom doesn't allow the cat to be in my room."

"How come?" Audra asked.

"She just doesn't, that's all." Rachel bent down and snatched Cuddles from Audra. Then she opened the back door and set the cat on the porch.

Audra picked up her backpack off the floor and followed Rachel upstairs.

When they entered Rachel's room, Rachel took a seat on the end of her bed. Audra set her backpack next to Rachel. "I brought some things for us to play with," she said.

Rachel tipped her head. "You knew you were coming over here today?"

Audra nodded. "Oh jah. Your mamm talked to my mamm when she saw her at the store last week. She invited us to come over and visit sometime soon. Mama thought today was as good a time as any, but then we got here and found out you weren't at home."

"I went to see my Grandma and Grandpa Yoder, but they weren't at home," Rachel said. "So I visited with my Aunt Karen and her little boy." Rachel chose not to mention that Gerald poked her in the eye. Audra might think it was funny or make fun of Rachel because she'd been down on her knees giving Gerald a horsey ride.

Audra opened the backpack and removed a yo-yo, a set of jacks, some crayons, and a coloring book. "What should we do first?"

Rachel stared at the things Audra had laid out on her bed. She wasn't in the mood to play with any of them. "How about a game of Scrabble?" she suggested. Rachel was good at spelling and making big words. She figured she could win the game easily.

"Jah, okay," Audra said with a shrug.

Rachel went to her closet and got out the Scrabble board. She placed it on the bed, and then she and Audra took seats on either side of the board. Audra went first, spelling the word *flower*. Using the letter *F*, going up and down, Rachel spelled the word *farmer*.

They continued to play until Rachel spelled the word *zephyr*, using squares that awarded double points.

Audra squinted at the board. "There's no such word as *zephyr*. You cheated, Rachel."

"Did not."

"Did so."

"Did not, and I'll prove it to you." Rachel hopped off the bed and scurried over to her desk. She kept a dictionary in the bottom drawer and knew it would prove there was such a word as *zephyr*. She brought it back to the bed and opened it to the section for the letter

Z. "See, it's right here," she said, pointing to the word. "Zephyr: The west wind. A soft, gentle breeze."

Audra pursed her lips.

Ha! Rachel knew her unexpected guest couldn't argue with the dictionary.

"I don't want to play this game anymore," Audra said. "Let's do something else."

"Like what?"

Audra pointed to the dresser across the room where the faceless doll Mary had given Rachel sat. "I'd like to play with her."

"My best friend gave me that faceless doll before she moved away," Rachel said. "I won't let anyone play with it but me."

Audra thrust out her bottom lip. "Why not?"

"Because the doll is special, and I don't want it to get ruined."

"Please, Rachel. I just want to hold her," Audra pleaded.

Rachel shook her head.

"I think you're being selfish."

Rachel was about to respond, when Mom called from the foot of the stairs, "I've set some cookies and milk on the kitchen table. Anyone who would like some, come on down!"

"Do you want some milk and cookies?" Rachel asked Audra.

Audra nodded. "That's sounds good."

"Then let's go."

"You go ahead," Audra said. "I'll be down as soon as I put my toys in my backpack."

"See you downstairs then." Rachel skipped out of the room and knocked on Jacob's bedroom door.

"Who is it?" he called.

"It's me, Rachel. Did you hear Mom say there are cookies and milk downstairs?"

"Jah, I did. Brian and I will be down in a minute."

"Okay." Rachel tromped down the stairs. She wished she didn't have to sit in the kitchen and eat cookies with Audra. She wished Audra's mother would say it was time for her, Audra, and Brian to go home.

Rachel flopped into a chair.

"Where are Audra and the boys?" Mom asked.

"They'll be down soon," Rachel replied.

A few moments later Audra took a seat at the table, hooking the straps of her backpack around the back of her chair.

Mom passed Audra the plate of cookies, and then she handed it to Rachel.

S-c-r-e-e-c-h. The back door creaked open.

"Levi, is that you?" Mom called over her shoulder.

"No, it's Jacob. Brian and I are going outside for a minute," Jacob said, poking his head inside the kitchen door.

"Don't you want some cookies and milk?"

"We'll have some when we come back in. I want Brian to meet Buddy." Jacob disappeared and the back door slammed shut.

Mom and Naomi visited while they sipped tea and ate cookies. Audra dunked a cookie in her glass of milk and looked at the door. "Can we go home now?" she asked her mother.

Naomi shook her head. "Not until Brian comes inside and has some cookies."

Audra fidgeted in her chair. *She seems kind of nervous,* Rachel thought. *Maybe she wants to go home just as much as I want her to leave.*

Rachel kept looking at the clock. Five minutes passed. Then ten more minutes went by. Finally, the boys entered the kitchen and took seats at the table. They each ate five cookies and drank two glasses of milk.

"I think it's time for us to go," Naomi said.

Rachel breathed a sigh of relief. *Finally.*

Audra's mother gave Mom a hug and said Mom should come visit her soon. It was obvious that she and Mom were already becoming friends.

It's fine with me if Mom wants to have Naomi as a friend, Rachel thought as she watched the Burkholders drive away in their buggy. *I just hope she doesn't expect me to be Audra's friend. I could never be friends with someone who accuses me of cheating at Scrabble.*

Rachel set her empty glass in the sink and walked up the steps to her room. She decided she would get her book on flowers and take it to Grandpa's room so they could talk about the things he wanted to grow in his greenhouse.

When Rachel entered her room, she opened the

bottom drawer of her dresser and removed the book. As she shut the drawer, she glanced at the top of the dresser and blinked. Something was wrong. Something was missing.

Rachel's heart pounded like a galloping horse, and she pressed the palm of her hand to her forehead. "My faceless doll is missing!" she gasped. "I'll bet anything that Audra took it!"

Chapter 5

A Shocking Discovery

Audra took my doll!" Rachel wailed when she ran into the kitchen where Mom was slicing some apples at the table.

Mom's glasses had slipped to the end of her nose, like they often did because the bridge of her nose was too narrow. She pushed them back in place and stared at Rachel like she'd lost her mind. "What are you talking about?"

"The faceless doll Mary gave me—it's missing." Rachel sniffed and swallowed around the lump clogging her throat. "When I came downstairs earlier for cookies and milk I left Audra alone in my room so she could pick up her toys. The—the doll was there before, but now it's gone, and I'm sure Audra took it!"

"Calm down, Rachel, and come have a seat." Mom motioned to the chair beside her. "You do tend to be kind of forgetful sometimes. You probably misplaced the doll."

Rachel shook her head. "No, no—I didn't! The doll was sitting on top of my dresser. That's where I put it after Mary gave it to me."

"Have you taken the doll down to play with it since Mary left?" Mom asked.

"I—I held it a few times, but I always put it right back on the dresser." Rachel frowned. "Audra saw it there and asked if she could play with it."

"Did she play with it?"

Rachel flopped into the chair. "No way! I told her it was a gift from my best friend and that I wouldn't let anyone play with it but me."

"That was rather selfish, don't you think?"

Rachel stared at the table as her eyes filled with tears. "The doll is all I have to remember Mary. I was afraid Audra might ruin it."

"I'm sure she wouldn't have ruined it with you sitting right there." Mom patted Rachel's arm. "Maybe Audra decided to play with the doll for a few minutes before she came downstairs for cookies and milk. She could have put the doll somewhere else in your room."

Rachel sniffed. "I looked everywhere. I'll bet Audra stuffed my doll into her backpack with the toys she brought so no one would see her sneak it out of the house."

"What reason would Audra have for taking your doll?"

"Because she doesn't like me. I told you that before."

"She brought her toys over here so she could play

with you today," Mom reminded Rachel. "I don't think she would have done that if she didn't like you."

"Audra's mamm probably told her to bring some toys." Rachel frowned and crossed her arms. "Besides, Audra accused me of cheating at Scrabble, and she's been mean to me at school."

Mom reached for an apple from the bowl sitting in the center of the table. "I think you're being unfair to Audra. You're not giving yourself a chance to like her, and you're not giving her a chance to be your friend."

"I don't want Audra to be my friend. I want Mary back—and that's it!" Rachel jumped up and raced out the back door. Mom didn't understand the way she felt; no one did. Grownups often forgot what it was like to be a kid.

Rachel ran to the barn to look for Cuddles. Maybe if she held the cat and petted her it would make her feel better. When Rachel was trapped in their neighbors' cellar last summer, Cuddles had comforted her, even though she was only a tiny kitten then.

When Rachel entered the barn, she was greeted by a musty odor coming from the leftover winter hay stacked against one wall. She didn't mind the smell, though. She liked being in the barn where the horses and cows were kept.

Rachel found Cuddles lying on a bale of hay, purring and licking her paws. She took a seat beside the cat so she could think. "You don't have a care in the world, Cuddles. It's me who has all the troubles." Rachel picked up the cat and held it in her lap. "What I'd like to know is how you could let Audra hold you and pet you? Don't you care that she's not my friend?"

Cuddles responded with a lazy, *meow!* Then she licked Rachel's hand with her warm, sandpapery tongue.

Rachel rubbed Cuddles behind one ear as she leaned her head against the wall and closed her eyes. She wanted to go over to Audra's house right now and ask for her doll back. She knew where Audra lived, too, because Audra had mentioned what road their house was on.

Maybe I'll go inside and ask Mom if I can go for a walk, Rachel thought. *Jah, that's just what I need to do.*

Rachel opened her eyes, set Cuddles on the hay next to her, and was about to get up when she spotted something dangling from the hayloft overhead. She gasped. "Ach! That's my faceless doll hanging by one arm!"

"Heh. . .heh. . .heh." Rachel heard snickering coming from somewhere high up in the barn. "Jacob Yoder is that you up there?"

Jacob poked his head out from behind a mound of hay in the loft and grinned. "How'd you like my little surprise, Rachel?"

She shook her finger at him and scowled. "I don't think your *little surprise* is one bit funny! You'd better get my doll down from there, *schnell* [quickly]!"

"Jah, okay. You don't have to get so worked up about it." Jacob untied the rope and let the doll loose.

Rachel held her breath as the doll dropped from the

hayloft. She reached for it but missed. The poor little doll landed facedown on the floor!

"My faceless doll had better not be ruined!" Rachel shouted. She scooped the doll into her arms and checked it over, front and back. Lucky for Jacob there were no rips in the cloth body or the doll's clothes. Since the doll had landed in a clump of hay, it wasn't even dirty.

"How did you get my doll?" Rachel called up to Jacob. "And why'd you hang it in the hayloft like that?"

Jacob scrambled down the ladder and marched up to Rachel. "I took it from your room after you and Audra went downstairs for cookies and milk." He wrinkled his nose and squinted at her. "Figured I'd teach you a lesson for being so moody and grumpy lately."

Rachel's chin trembled and tears stung the backs of her eyes. "You'd be grumpy and moody, too, if your best friend moved away." She held the doll close and sniffed a couple of times. "This little faceless doll is all I have to remember Mary by."

"Aw, come on, Rachel. You're not going to cry, are you?" Jacob touched her arm. "I'm sorry for hanging your doll in the hayloft. I was only teasing. I didn't think you'd get so upset."

"I don't think you're really sorry, Jacob. All you ever do is tease and make fun of me. I'm getting sick and tired of it!" Rachel pushed Jacob's hand away and rushed out of the barn.

When Rachel entered the house a few moments later, she held her doll out to Mom and said, "I found it!"

Mom smiled. "Was it in your room?"

Rachel shook her head. "It was in the barn—hanging by one arm from the hayloft!"

Mom's eyebrows furrowed. "How did it get up there?"

"Jacob did it!"

"Why would Jacob take your doll?"

"He said it was to teach me a lesson because I've been moody and grumpy lately."

"Jacob shouldn't have taken your doll," Mom said with a shake of her head, "but he's right about you acting moody and grumpy. You've been that way ever since Mary and her family moved to Indiana."

Rachel stared at the floor as her eyes flooded with tears. "I can't help it. I miss Mary something awful." *Sniff. Sniff.* "I don't think I'll ever forgive Uncle Ben for taking her away."

"I know you miss your cousin, but that's no reason to be grumpy or unforgiving with others. Mary's daed did what he thought was best for him and his family, and he has a new job that he really enjoys." Mom pulled Rachel to her side and gave her a hug. "I'll have a talk with Jacob about what he did to your doll, but I want you to think about the things I've said and what you might do to improve your attitude."

Rachel nodded slowly. "All right, Mom."

Rachel spent the next hour lying on her bed, holding her faceless doll in her arms, tears trickling down her cheeks. Having the doll close made her feel a little closer to Mary.

She squeezed her eyes shut, trying to stop the flow of tears. *I wonder why Mary hasn't written to me yet. Has she forgotten about me? Has she found another friend she likes better? Maybe I should write a letter to her now and find out why she hasn't written.*

Rachel heard laughter coming from the backyard, and her eyes popped open. She dried her eyes with the back of her hand, climbed off the bed, and hurried over to the window. Orlie stood beside Jacob in front of Buddy's new dog run, pointing at Buddy. He said something to Jacob that Rachel couldn't understand, even though her window was slightly open.

Rachel rolled her eyes. That smelly mutt was lying on top of his dog house with his head between his dirty paws!

Orlie looked up toward Rachel's open window and waved at her. Jacob looked up and waved, too. "Come out and join us, Rachel!" Orlie shouted with his hands cupped around his mouth.

Rachel blew out a big puff of air. The last thing she wanted to do was be with Orlie or Jacob right now. But if she didn't go outside, Jacob would probably tell Mom she was being moody and grumpy again.

Rachel set the faceless doll on her dresser and headed downstairs.

"*Wie geht's?* [How are you?]" Orlie asked when Rachel joined him and Jacob in front of the dog run a few minutes later.

"I've been better," she said, squinting at Jacob.

Jacob squinted right back at her and said, "I was just telling Orlie that ever since Pap built the doghouse, Buddy won't sleep in it. Instead, he sleeps on the roof."

Rachel snickered as she shook her head. "That dog of yours is so dumm."

"He's not dumb." Jacob motioned to Buddy, who was now snoring and grunting in his sleep. "He's just different, that's all."

Rachel looked over at Orlie. "Did Buddy do weird things when he lived with you?"

Orlie shrugged. "Sometimes, but I guess all dogs do some weird things."

"Just like people," Jacob muttered under his breath.

Rachel bumped Jacob's arm. "What was that?"

"Oh, nothing."

"So, Jacob, how is Buddy's training coming along?" Orlie asked.

"Not so well," Jacob replied. "He doesn't respond to the new whistle I bought him. In fact, whenever I blow it, all he does is howl."

"Why don't I try the whistle and see if it works for me?" Orlie suggested.

"Okay. Let me get Buddy out of the pen." Jacob opened the door of the dog run and called, "Here, Buddy. Come on out and see Orlie."

Buddy's eyes opened and his head snapped up in attention. His ears flicked forward. His tail wagged. He leaped off the doghouse and raced toward Rachel.

"Ach!" Rachel jumped back, but it was too late.

Slurp, slurp, slurp. Buddy swiped his long pink tongue across Rachel's arm.

"Yuck!" She pushed the dog away and scowled at Jacob. "That dog of yours has horrible breath!"

"He's a dog. What do you expect?"

"Maybe you should brush his teeth."

Jacob ignored Rachel's last comment and reached into his pants pocket. He pulled out the plastic whistle he'd been using to train Buddy and handed it to Orlie. "Here you go."

Orlie put the whistle between his lips and blew. *Whee. . .whee. . .whee.*

Rachel gritted her teeth and covered her ears, knowing what would come next.

Buddy leaned his head way back and howled.

Orlie stood there with a confused look on his face. "This isn't the right kind of whistle. The whistle I had for Buddy was a silent whistle—the kind only a dog can hear."

Jacob rubbed his chin. "Hmm. . .guess I'll have to save up my money so I can buy one of those silent whistles."

"Either that or you can keep working with Buddy on your own." Orlie patted Buddy's head. "If you work with him long enough, I'm sure he'll begin to understand and start obeying your commands."

Rachel grunted. "I don't think Jacob could say or do anything that would make Buddy mind. That dog's just a dumm mutt."

"No, he's not." Jacob shook his head. "He's a good dog—a smart dog, and I'm sure he can be trained."

"I'll believe it when I see it." Rachel motioned to the house. "I'm going to the kitchen to see if there's anything good to eat. Are you two coming?"

"I think we'll work with Buddy awhile," Jacob said. "We'll be up in a little bit."

"Suit yourself." Rachel sprinted across the lawn, anxious to get to the house before Buddy decided to give her more kisses with his slimy tongue.

When Rachel entered the kitchen, she was pleased to see Grandpa sitting at the table reading a magazine.

"How's your back doing today, Grandpa?" she asked. "Are you any feeling better?"

He nodded. "At least I can stand up straight when I walk now. Of course, it'll be some time before I'm able to work in the garden or do any lifting."

"You shouldn't lift anything heavy," Mom said as she set a plate of ginger cookies on the table. She smiled at Rachel. "I did more baking today. Would you like to join Grandpa and me for cookies and milk?"

Rachel nodded. "That sounds good."

Mom motioned to the window. "I see Orlie Troyer out there with Jacob. Why don't you call them inside for some cookies, Rachel?"

"They're playing with Buddy. Jacob said they might be in later." Rachel pulled out the chair beside Grandpa and sat down. "Orlie told Jacob that the whistle he's been using to train Buddy is the wrong kind. He should have been using a silent whistle, not a whistle that blows so loudly it hurts people's ears."

"It probably hurts Buddy's ears, too." Grandpa reached for a cookie. "No wonder that poor dog howls so much."

"I wish Jacob would get rid of Buddy." Rachel frowned. "He's nothing but trouble."

"I think the dog's doing better now that he has his own dog run." Mom set some glasses on the table, along with a jug of cold milk. "With a little more work, I'm sure Buddy will be just fine."

"Humph!" Rachel folded her arms. "He'll probably never stop chasing Cuddles."

Mom poured milk into the glasses and clucked her tongue. "I wish you wouldn't be so negative, Rachel."

Rachel grabbed a cookie and dunked it in her milk. It was easy for Mom to be positive about Buddy. The beast never tried to kiss Mom. He saved his slurpy kisses just for Rachel!

After Rachel ate three cookies and finished her milk, Mom looked at her and said, "Since the boys haven't come in yet, why don't you take a tray of cookies and milk out to the porch for them?"

Rachel wrinkled her nose. "Do I have to?"

Mom nodded. "I think it would be a nice thing to do."

Rachel didn't feel like doing anything nice for Jacob, but she knew better than to argue with Mom. "Okay," she said, rising from her seat.

Mom put two glasses of milk and a plate of cookies

on a tray and handed it to Rachel. Then she pushed the screen door open and held it while Rachel stepped outside.

Rachel was about to the set the tray on the small table on the porch when—*whack!*—Orlie dashed onto the porch right behind Buddy and bumped Rachel's arm. The tray slipped out of her hands and crashed to the floor, spilling milk and cookies all over Rachel's dress and her sneakers.

"Look what you did!" Rachel shouted.

"I–I'm sorry," Orlie stammered.

"You bumped into me on purpose!"

"I was chasing after Buddy and didn't see you—"

Without waiting for Orlie to finish his sentence, Rachel jerked open the screen door and dashed into the house. "Always trouble somewhere," she grumbled.

Chapter 6

Another Rotten Day

When Rachel arrived at school on Monday morning, she spotted Orlie standing near the swings—talking to Audra!

Rachel frowned. She still hadn't forgiven Orlie for bumping into her on Saturday and spilling milk all over her dress and sneakers. Even though Rachel knew Audra hadn't taken her doll, she was still angry with Audra for accusing her of cheating at Scrabble, for splattering mud on her dress, and for eating her peanut butter and jelly sandwich.

Rachel crossed her arms when she saw Orlie hand Audra an apple. She thought of the day Orlie gave her an apple with a big fat worm inside. He claimed he didn't know the worm was there, but she was sure he'd given her that wormy apple on purpose.

She clenched her hands into tight little balls. *I'll bet the apple he gave Audra doesn't have a worm in it. I'll bet Orlie likes Audra more than he likes me.*

"What are you looking at, and how come you're wearing such a sour look on your face?" Jacob asked, nudging Rachel with his elbow.

"I'm not looking at anything important." Rachel stretched her lips into a wide, fake smile. "And I was not wearing a sour look."

"Jah, you were." Jacob nudged her again. "And take that silly grin off your face. It doesn't look real."

"Just leave me alone," Rachel grumbled as she started up the schoolhouse stairs.

"Elizabeth hasn't rung the bell yet," Jacob called after her.

"I don't care." Rachel opened the door and went inside. She had just put her lunch pail on the shelf when Elizabeth walked by and said, "Couldn't wait for the bell, huh, Rachel?"

Rachel only shrugged in reply.

"Go ahead and take your seat," Elizabeth said. "I'm sure the others will be in as soon as I ring the bell."

Rachel flopped into the chair at her desk. She took out her pencil and paper when Orlie entered and took a seat at the desk in front of her. "Was your mamm mad about the milk you got on your dress the other day?" he asked.

She frowned. "*I* didn't get the milk on my dress. *You* bumped into me, so it was *your* fault my dress and sneakers got covered with milk."

"It was an accident. I told you I was sorry."

Rachel placed her hands on her desk and stared

straight ahead. She wasn't interested in anything Orlie had to say.

"Good morning boys and girls," Elizabeth said as she took a seat at her desk.

"Good morning, Elizabeth," Rachel said along with the other children.

"I'll be reading Matthew 18:21–22," Elizabeth said as she opened her Bible. "Then Peter came to Jesus and asked, 'Lord, how many times shall I forgive my brother when he sins against me? Up to seven times?' Jesus answered, 'I tell you, not seven times, but seventy-seven times.'"

Rachel was tempted to bite off a fingernail, but she picked up her pencil and stuck it between her teeth instead. Seventy-seven times? That seemed impossible! Maybe the verse was talking about good friends, like Mary. If Mary had said or done something to hurt Rachel, it would be easy to forgive her—but not Orlie or Audra, who weren't even her friends.

As Rachel stood with the other children to recite the Lord's Prayer, she glanced across the aisle at Audra's desk. There sat the big red apple Orlie had given her.

Rachel barely heard the words being recited by her classmates. All she could think about was how miserable she felt without Mary. During singing time, Rachel struggled to sing along.

When the children finished the last song and were about to return to their seats—*whoosh!*—a sparrow swooped into the room through an open window.

Some of the children screamed and ran to hide under their desks. Others darted around the room, laughing and trying to catch the little bird. Rachel just stood there, wishing there was something she could do to rescue the poor creature.

Aaron and Orlie bumped heads as they lunged for the sparrow at the same time.

The bird swooped past Jacob. He raced after it, tripped on Phoebe's foot, and fell flat on his face.

"Scholars, back to your desks, schnell!" Elizabeth clapped her hands, and everyone raced to their seats.

Rachel had just sat down when—*floop*—the little bird landed right on her head! She sat there a few seconds to see what the bird would do and was surprised when it didn't fly away. Maybe it needed a friend as much as she did.

The room got quiet as everyone stared at Rachel. Slowly she raised her hands and lifted the sparrow off her head. Then she walked to the back of the room, opened the door, and stepped onto the porch to let the bird go.

Rachel smiled as she watched the sparrow fly up to a tree. *At least I know someone likes me today.*

Rachel was in a better mood by the time she got home from school that afternoon. After the sparrow landed on her head and she set him free outdoors, the rest of the day had gone better. Everyone said how special they thought it was that the little bird landed on her head. Everyone but Audra, that is. She hadn't said a word to Rachel all day. Well, that was fine with Rachel. She didn't like talking to Audra anyway.

"I think I'll ride my skateboard in the barn," Rachel told Jacob as they entered their yard. "I checked there last night, and the floor in the main part of the barn is clear of hay."

Jacob shook his head. "As many times as you've fallen on that skateboard, I'm surprised you still ride it."

"As our teacher always says, 'Practice makes perfect.' "

"Jah, well, you can practice riding your skateboard if you want to, but I'm going to work with Buddy."

Rachel put her hands on her hips and squinted at Jacob. "You'd better not let that mutt in the barn while I'm skateboarding."

Jacob shook his head. "Don't worry. We'll stay in the yard."

"Good." Rachel tromped up the steps and entered the house. She glanced in the kitchen, but there was no sign of Mom. Maybe she was in the living room.

Rachel looked in the living room, but Mom wasn't there, either. She was probably in her room taking a nap. Mom took lots of naps now that she was expecting a baby.

Rachel hurried upstairs and changed out of her school dress into one of the dresses she wore for playing and doing chores. Then she rushed downstairs and out the door.

When Rachel entered the barn, she headed straight for the shelf where she kept her skateboard. She carried it to the part of the barn where the hay had been cleared. Buddy was nowhere to be seen, so Rachel thought it'd be fun to give Cuddles a ride on her skateboard.

Rachel cupped her hands around her mouth and called, "Here, Cuddles! Come, kitty, kitty."

Cuddles stuck her head out from behind a bale of hay. *Meow!*

Rachel clapped her hands. "Come here, Cuddles. Let's go for a ride on my skateboard."

Meow! Meow! Cuddles darted behind the bale of hay.

"All right then," Rachel said with a shrug, "if you don't want to go for a ride, I'll have all the fun myself." She stepped onto her skateboard with her right foot, pushed off with her left foot, and sailed across the barn floor. "*Whee*. . .this is so much fun! You don't know what you're missing, Cuddles."

Rachel turned and headed back across the barn on her skateboard. The barn door opened and Henry stepped in. At the same time, Cuddles darted out from behind the bale of hay and zipped right in front of Henry.

"Look out for my cat!" Rachel shouted. It was too late—Henry stepped right on Cuddles's tail!

Mee-ow! Cuddles screeched, and her ears went straight back. Then she darted across the floor in front of Rachel.

Rachel swerved to miss hitting the cat, but her skateboard tipped and fell to the floor with a crash.

"Ouch! Ouch! Ouch!" Rachel tried not to cry, but her

knees started to bleed and they hurt something awful.

"Rachel, are you hurt?" Henry asked, rushing to her side.

She nodded and touched her skinned knees. "You should have watched where you were going."

"I'm sorry," said Henry as he helped Rachel to her feet. "I never expected your cat to run in front of me like that."

Rachel's chin trembled and her eyes filled with tears. "Look at my dress!" she wailed, pointing to an ugly tear in the skirt. "Mom's gonna be awful mad when she sees this. If you hadn't stepped on Cuddles's tail, it wouldn't have happened."

"How do you know that?" Henry motioned to Cuddles, who lay curled on a patch of straw, licking her paws. "That *narrisch* [crazy] cat of yours could have raced in front of your skateboard and caused you to fall even if I hadn't stepped on her tail."

Rachel frowned. "You're not sorry for making me fall. You're trying to put the blame on Cuddles." She whirled around and raced out of the barn.

When Rachel stepped into the kitchen a few moments later, she found Mom sitting at the table drinking a cup of tea.

"Rachel, your dress—and your knees!" Mom exclaimed. "What in the world happened?"

Rachel told Mom what happened, and she ended it by saying, "I'm really mad at Henry for what he did!"

"Did Henry apologize?" Mom asked.

Rachel nodded. "But I don't think he meant it."

"I'm sure Henry didn't purposely step on the cat's tail. You need to forgive your brother."

Rachel stared at the floor.

Mom left her seat, opened a cupboard door, and took out a box of bandages and some antiseptic. Rachel took a seat at the table and stuck out both legs.

"Does it hurt much?" Mom asked as she dabbed some of the medicine on Rachel's knees.

"A little."

When Mom finished bandaging Rachel's knees she said, "Run upstairs now and change out of your dress. When you come down, you can mend your dress."

Rachel swallowed around the lump in her throat. "I don't see why I have to fix the hole in my dress. It was Henry's fault that it tore."

Mom squinted at Rachel over the top of her glasses. "As I said before, I don't think Henry stepped on Cuddles's tail on purpose. Now do as I say and run upstairs to change your dress."

Rachel trudged up the stairs, mumbling, "I don't think anyone likes me."

Rachel changed into a clean dress and was walking down the stairs when—*whack!*—she heard something hit the living room window. Rachel raced into the room and looked out the window. Lying in the flowerbed was a baby robin with its feet in the air. Rachel dropped her torn dress on a chair and raced outside. She had reached the spot where the bird lay, when Cuddles streaked across the yard, heading straight for the helpless little bird.

"No, Cuddles!" Rachel quickly picked up the bird. Relieved to see that it was still breathing, she set it on one of their bird feeders. "Don't worry, little birdie," she said. "You'll be okay. I'm sure you'll be able to fly again."

Rachel dashed into the house. "Mom, Mom!" she shouted as she raced into the kitchen. "A baby robin hit the living room window, and it was lying in the flowerbed with its feet in the air. I rescued the poor thing and put it on one of our bird feeders."

"Are you sure the bird wasn't dead?" Mom asked. "Hitting the window like that could have done in a baby bird."

Rachel shook her head. "No, no, I'm sure it was still breathing. I'm going back outside to check on it." She ran back outside and over to the feeder. She was happy to see that the little bird was still there, and it was breathing!

"Come on, little birdie, fly away, fly away." Rachel stared at the bird, hoping it would fly.

Suddenly, the bird opened its eyes, looked right at Rachel, and flew high into the tree.

Rachel smiled. This was the second time today that she'd rescued a bird, and she felt really good about that. In fact, helping her little bird friends had made her feel better about her otherwise rotten day.

She wished she could tell Mary about the two birds

she had helped. Maybe this was a good time to write that letter to Mary she'd been meaning to write.

Rachel hurried into the house and went straight to her room. She took a seat at her desk and got out a piece of paper and a pencil. Then she began writing the letter.

Dear Mary,

I've been waiting to hear from you ever since you moved, and I don't understand why I haven't gotten a letter yet.

Have you been busy unpacking? I've been busy here, too. Grandpa hurt his back the other day, but he's doing better now.

There's a new girl at school. Her name is Audra, and Elizabeth gave her your desk. Audra's been mean to me, and it doesn't seem right for her to be sitting in your desk.

Something good happened today, though. A bird got into the schoolhouse and no one could catch it. Then the bird landed on my head, and everyone was surprised when I picked it up and took it outside.

When I got home from school today, a bird hit our window and landed in the flowerbed. I thought it might be dead, but I set it on a bird feeder, and when I checked on it again, it was okay and flew into the tree.

Rachel stopped writing for a moment when a lump

formed in her throat. She should have been telling Mary all these things in person—not writing them in a letter.

"Oh, Mary, I miss you so much. Please write back to me."

Chapter 7

Chain of Events

As Rachel entered the schoolyard the following morning, she spotted Orlie talking with Audra again. They were grinning like a couple of little kids with a sack full of candy. Rachel noticed that Orlie held Audra's backpack, as well as his own.

Rachel kicked at a stone with the toe of her sneaker. *I knew it. Orlie does like Audra better than me. He probably walked her to school this morning.*

Rachel wasn't sure why she cared so much. It wasn't as if she and Orlie were best friends or anything. Only Mary had been Rachel's best friend, but now Rachel had no friends at all.

"I don't care," she mumbled under her breath. "I don't need any friends."

"What was that, Rachel?" Jacob asked.

"Nothing."

"You said something. I heard you."

"It was nothing important, and I wasn't talking to you, anyway."

"Who were you talking to, little bensel?"

"I was talking to myself." Rachel whirled around. "And stop calling me that! I'm getting tired of you picking on me all the time."

"I'm just teasing." Jacob wrinkled his nose. "Can't you even take a joke?"

Rachel didn't answer. Instead, she plodded up the schoolhouse steps and hurried inside.

"You're the first one in class again," Elizabeth said when Rachel took a seat behind her desk a few minutes later. "You must really like being in school. Maybe you'll grow up to be a teacher like me some day."

Rachel pursed her lips. She hadn't even thought of what she'd like to do when she grew up. Maybe becoming a schoolteacher wouldn't be a bad idea. It would be better than getting married like her sister, Esther, had done. On the other hand, Esther seemed really happy being married to Rudy. Now that they were expecting a baby, Esther had a smile on her face all the time.

"So what do you think, Rachel?" Elizabeth asked. "Would you like to be a schoolteacher someday?"

Rachel shrugged. "Maybe."

Elizabeth smiled and patted Rachel's shoulder. "I guess I'd better ring the school bell now."

"I want everyone to play baseball," Elizabeth announced before dismissing the class for their noontime recess. "It's a beautiful spring day, and the fresh air and exercise will be good for us all."

Rachel frowned. She wanted to swing—not play baseball during recess.

Even though she enjoyed doing lots of outdoor games, playing baseball was not one of her favorite things to do.

"Let's play the boys against the girls!" Aaron shouted.

"No way," said Phoebe. "There are too many good boy players, so it wouldn't be fair if all the boys were on one team."

"I agree," Audra spoke up.

"I'll decide who will be on each team," Elizabeth said. "I'll also play on one of the teams, and my helper, Sharon, will be on the other."

Elizabeth soon had the children divided into two teams, and everyone took their place. Rachel was glad she wasn't on Orlie's team, but it didn't make her happy to see that Audra was on his team.

Rachel's team was up first, with Rachel first in line to bat. With a sense of determination, she stepped up to the plate. Gripping the bat and clenching her teeth, she waited for Orlie to pitch the ball.

He smiled at Rachel, gave a quick nod, and—whizz!—the ball zipped over home plate. Rachel swung hard but missed.

"Strike one!" Elizabeth hollered.

Orlie pitched another ball to Rachel, and she missed again, the weight of the bat spinning her around in a circle.

"Strike two!"

Rachel knew she only had one more strike left, and then she'd be out. She couldn't let that happen. She had to hit the ball and make it to first base—maybe two or three bases—maybe even make a homerun!

She took her stance, holding the bat firm and steady. The pitch came fast, and—*whack!*—she smacked it out into left field!

Rachel dropped the bat to the ground and took off running. She ran so fast her kapp strings waved behind her like streamers. She sprinted to first base and kept on running.

She heard Orlie holler, "Catch that ball, Audra! Tag Rachel out!"

Rachel kept running—past second base and heading for third. She was going to make it—maybe all the way home!

Rachel saw a white blur out of the corner of her eye, and then Audra leaping into the air. *Thwack!* The ball thunked Rachel right on the nose!

"Ach, my *naas* [nose]!" Rachel nearly gagged when she felt something drip down her throat—a strange, metallic taste. She touched the end of her nose, and when she looked at her fingers, there was blood on them.

Orlie rushed forward. "I'm sorry, Rachel. I thought Audra was gonna catch the ball."

"I tried to catch the ball, but it came too fast." Audra stared at Rachel and squinted. "I hope your naas isn't broken. It looks kind of swollen."

Elizabeth rushed up to Rachel and covered her nose with a tissue. "You'd better come inside with me so I can get the bleeding stopped."

With tears stinging her eyes and her nose throbbing like crazy, Rachel followed her teacher into the schoolhouse.

"Take a seat at your desk, and I'll get some cold water and a clean cloth," Elizabeth instructed. "In the meantime, keep that tissue over your nose."

Rachel did as her teacher said, trying not to give in to the threatening tears pushing against her eyelids. *I'll bet Orlie threw that ball so it would hit me in the nose,* she fumed. *Audra probably missed it on purpose, too.*

Elizabeth returned to Rachel's desk and placed a cold cloth on Rachel's nose and one on the back of her neck. "Let's see if that stops the bleeding," she said. "If it doesn't, I'll try some vinegar."

"Vinegar?" Rachel had never heard of anyone with a nosebleed having to drink vinegar.

"It's an old-time remedy," Elizabeth explained. "You put a little vinegar on the end of a tissue and stick it up your nostril to stop the bleeding."

"That sounds awful." Rachel hoped her nose would stop bleeding on its own. It was one thing to eat something that had vinegar in it, like pickled beets or dill pickles, but putting vinegar up her nose didn't sound fun at all. She was sure it would sting.

A few minutes later, Elizabeth came to check her nose. When she pulled the cloth aside, she smiled and said, "The bleeding has slowed. It should stop soon, I think."

Rachel breathed a sigh of relief. *No vinegar for me.*

By the time the others had come inside from recess, Rachel's nose had stopped bleeding.

"Are you all right?" Orlie asked as he took his seat in front of Rachel.

"My nose has stopped bleeding, but it still hurts," she said.

"You're not mad at me, I hope."

Rachel gave no reply.

Orlie shrugged and turned to face the front of the room.

Rachel took out her spelling book. Spelling was her favorite subject, and since she was the best speller in the third and fourth grades, she hoped she would feel better after they'd had their spelling bee.

While Rachel waited for the teacher to get things ready, she studied the list of spelling words: *address, blister, cavity, disturb, entry, faithful, gelatin. . .* She knew how to spell every word on the page and should be able to easily win the class spelling bee.

She glanced across the aisle. Audra was studying her spelling words, too. Could Audra spell well? She didn't like bugs and couldn't play baseball very well. Maybe Audra liked spelling and would be hard to beat. She'd played Scrabble fairly well—until she'd accused Rachel of cheating. Maybe. . .

"All right, scholars," Elizabeth said, rising from her

desk, "this is how we're going to do our spelling bee today." She motioned to the front of the room. "Those of you in grades one and two will line up to receive your words first. When we have a winner from that group, the third and fourth graders will come up front, followed by the fifth and sixth graders. Our seventh and eighth graders will go last."

Rachel was glad the first and second graders were going first. That gave her more time to study her list of spelling words. Of course, she didn't know which of the words on the list Elizabeth would ask, but she wasn't worried. In fact, she figured the spelling bee would be the best part of her day.

It didn't take long until the first and second graders were done. Danny Fisher was the last scholar standing, and he got to put a yellow star on the first and second grader's section of the wall. Then he got to choose one of the new fiction books Elizabeth had brought to school today. Sharon gave all the first and second graders a piece of candy from a basket on her desk.

"Now it's time for the third and fourth graders to take their places," Elizabeth said.

Rachel hopped up from her desk and made her way to the front of the room. She squeezed into a spot between Orlie and Audra. *At least they aren't standing together this time.*

Elizabeth started at the end of the line, giving the first word, *street*, to Nona Lapp.

That's an easy word, Rachel thought. *I could spell*

"street" when I was in the first grade.

Nona spelled the word correctly, and Elizabeth continued down the line. When she came to Orlie she gave him the word *walnut.* Orlie rubbed his chin and squinted his eyes. "Hmm. . .let me think."

"The word is *walnut,*" Elizabeth repeated. "Can you spell it, Orlie?"

Orlie blinked a couple of times, and a silly grin came over his face. "Sure, I can spell *it. I-T.*"

Everyone laughed—except Elizabeth and Sharon.

Elizabeth frowned and said, "Orlie Troyer, do you want to stay after school today?"

He shook his head and stared at the floor. "No, Elizabeth."

"Then stop fooling around and spell the word *walnut* for us."

Orlie shifted from his right foot to his left foot and bit his lip nervously. Rachel could tell he was struggling and didn't know how to spell the word. She was tempted to whisper it to him but knew that would be cheating. Once, she cheated on a history test, and after that she promised never to cheat again.

Elizabeth tapped her foot against the hardwood floor. "We're waiting for your answer, Orlie."

Orlie cleared his throat a couple of times and finally lifted his head. "W-a-l-l-n-u-t. Walnut."

Rachel groaned inwardly, and Elizabeth shook her head. "That's incorrect. I'm sorry, Orlie, you'll have to take your seat."

With a bright smile, Orlie dashed back to his desk. It

seemed as if he was glad he had missed the word. Rachel knew spelling wasn't one of Orlie's best subjects. Maybe he was relieved that he didn't have to stand in front of the class and be embarrassed any longer. Now he could sit in his desk and wait for someone else to mess up.

I hope it's not me, Rachel thought. *I don't want to miss one single word. I want to win this spelling bee.*

"Rachel, did you hear what I said?"

Rachel jerked her head toward Elizabeth. She'd been so busy thinking about Orlie and how much she wanted to win that she hadn't heard what her teacher said.

"Uh. . .what was that?" she mumbled.

Everyone laughed, and Rachel's face heated up.

Elizabeth clucked her tongue. "Please spell the word *walnut.*"

Rachel nodded. "Walnut. W-a-l-n-u-t. Walnut."

"That's correct," Elizabeth said.

Rachel smiled, feeling quite pleased with herself.

Elizabeth faced Audra. "Your word is *windmill.*"

Rachel held her breath and waited to see if Audra could spell the word.

Audra smiled and said, "Windmill. W-i-n-d-m-i-l-l. Windmill."

"Correct."

I guess Audra's a good speller, Rachel thought. *Either that or it was a lucky guess.*

Elizabeth continued down the line, giving each of the students in the third and fourth grades a word. Some spelled their words correctly and others ended up taking their seats like Orlie. Elizabeth started at the beginning of the line again, and when it was Rachel's turn, she spelled her next word correctly. Audra spelled her word correctly, too.

On and on it went, until only two scholars were left standing—Rachel and Audra.

The next word went to Rachel. It was *harness.*

Rachel's heart went *thump. . .thump. . .thump.* "H-a-r-" She paused and drew in a quick breath. *I've got to get this right. I can't mess up now.*

"Do you know the word, Rachel?" Elizabeth asked.

Rachel started again. "H-a-r-n-e-s-s. Harness."

"That's correct."

Rachel breathed a sigh of relief.

Elizabeth faced Audra. "Your word is *oxygen.*"

Audra scratched her head. "Let's see now. . ."

"We're waiting, Audra," Elizabeth said.

Audra's forehead wrinkled and she pursed her lips. "O-x-y— No, the correct spelling is. . .uh—o-x-e-g-e-n."

Elizabeth shook her head. "I'm sorry, Audra, that's wrong."

Audra's face turned bright red. With head down and shoulders slumped, she shuffled to her desk.

"Rachel, you're the winner of the third and fourth grade spelling bee." Elizabeth handed Rachel a star to put on the wall and motioned to the basket on Sharon's desk. "Help yourself to a piece of candy."

Rachel took a stick of licorice then went to hang up her star. She felt really good about herself—maybe even full of a little *hochmut* [pride]. She remembered hearing their bishop say during church one day that it was wrong to be full of hochmut. "*We should be humble, never boastful,*" he said.

As Rachel put her star in place, she thought about the bishop's words. It was hard not to feel prideful sometimes—especially when she'd done something that made her feel so good. Maybe it was all right to feel good when she'd done something well. She just needed to be careful not to brag about it.

Rachel headed back to her desk. She was almost there when Audra turned sideways in her desk, and— *thump!*—Rachel tripped on Audra's foot and landed face-down on the floor!

Blood spurted out of Rachel's nose. "No, no! Not again!" she moaned. Why was it that every time things seemed to be going well, something happened to bring more trouble?

"Are you all right?" Elizabeth asked as she helped Rachel to her feet.

"My naas—it's bleeding." Rachel struggled not to cry as Elizabeth led her to the back of the schoolhouse where she kept a basin of water. Rachel sat on a stool while Elizabeth put wet cloths on her nose and the back of her neck.

"Audra tripped me on purpose," Rachel whimpered.

"Now, Rachel, why would Audra do that?"

"She's probably jealous because I won the spelling bee."

"Audra shouldn't have had her feet in the aisle," Elizabeth said, "but I don't think she tripped you on purpose."

Rachel folded her arms and sat there feeling sorry for herself. Why did everyone think Audra was so nice? Couldn't they see she was nothing but trouble?

Audra approached Rachel quietly, a worried expression on her face. "I'm sorry about your nose, Rachel," she said. "I turned in my seat so I could ask Orlie something and didn't see you coming down the aisle."

Rachel stared straight ahead.

Elizabeth touched Rachel's shoulder. "Aren't you going to accept Audra's apology?"

Rachel lifted her shoulders in a shrug.

"God tells us to forgive others when they apologize," Elizabeth said.

Rachel closed her eyes and prayed: *Lord, I still think Audra tripped me on purpose, but help me to forgive her and have a better attitude.*

She opened her eyes and mumbled, "I forgive you, Audra."

Elizabeth turned to Audra. "From now on, please keep your feet under your desk and not in the aisle."

"I will." Audra hurried back to her desk.

Rachel clenched her hands into fists to keep herself from biting a nail.

Chapter 8

Wishing Fishing

Would you like to do some wishing fishing with me today?" Grandpa asked Rachel on Saturday morning as she stood at the sink helping Mom do the dishes.

"What's wishing fishing?" Rachel asked, turning to face Grandpa.

He wiggled his bushy gray eyebrows. "Wishing fishing is when you drop your line into the water and sit there wishing you'll catch a big one."

Rachel giggled and dropped the sponge into the water, sending colorful bubbles to the ceiling. "Wishing fishing sounds like fun, Grandpa. Are you sure you're feeling up to it?"

"My back's doing better now. I think a day in the sunshine with my fishing pole is just what I need. Maybe it's what you need, too, Rachel."

"That's a good idea," said Mom as she reached into the drainer and plucked out a clean dish to dry. She looked at Rachel and smiled. "Your daed and Jacob left for town right after breakfast, and Henry's going over to see his girlfriend soon. You and Grandpa will have some time to be alone together today."

"What about you, Mom?" Rachel asked. "What are you going to do today?"

"I'm planning to sew some clothes for the boppli." Mom patted her round belly. "It won't be too many more months before our little one will be born, and he or she will need some clothes to wear."

Grandpa left the table and came to stand beside Rachel. "I'll bet you're getting excited about being a big *schweschder* [sister], jah?" he asked, squeezing her shoulder.

Rachel shrugged. She didn't want to think about becoming a big sister right now. She just wanted to think about going fishing with Grandpa.

Grandpa ambled across the room and plucked his straw hat from the wall peg where he'd hung it last night. "I'll go on out to the barn and get our fishing poles. Then I'll hitch a horse to one of your daed's buggies. When you're done with the dishes, come on out. " He looked over his shoulder and winked at her. Then he plopped his straw hat on his head. "It won't be long until we'll be doing some wishing fishing!"

"Ah, the Lord is so good!" Grandpa said as he and Rachel sat on a grassy spot on the shoreline of the pond. "Can you smell that fresh spring air?"

Rachel's nose twitched as she inhaled deeply. "Jah, it does smell kind of nice."

"Pretty soon there'll be wild flowers growing all around the pond." Grandpa smiled. "Those will smell nice, too."

Rachel nodded.

"Speaking of flowers," Grandpa said. "After you went to bed last night, I spoke with your daed about my greenhouse idea."

"What'd he say?"

"He agreed to help me build it near the front of his property."

"Oh, Grandpa, that's *wunderbaar* [wonderful]. When will it happen?"

"Probably sometime this spring." He patted her arm. "Maybe you'd like to help me in the greenhouse when you're not in school."

Rachel nodded happily. "I'd like that. I think being around all those flowers will be a lot of fun!" She removed her sneakers and wiggled her bare toes in the grass. It felt nice to be here with Grandpa, talking about his new greenhouse and getting ready to catch some fish. Today was turning out to be a pretty good day.

"Having a greenhouse will be fun," Grandpa said, "but it will also mean a lot of work."

"Working with flowers won't seem like work to me," Rachel said with a shake of her head.

Grandpa chuckled. "I guess we'll have to wait and see about that." He reached into his bag of fishing supplies and pulled out a can of worms. "Would you like me to bait your hook, Rachel?"

"That's all right. I can do it myself." Rachel reached into the can, plucked out a fat, wiggly worm, and baited her hook. Then she cast the line into the water.

Grandpa took a worm from the can and baited his hook. He drew his arm back, flicked his wrist, and—*swish*—Rachel's kapp lifted right off her head.

She looked up in shock at her hat as it dangled from the fishhook at the end of Grandpa's line. "Grandpa, what'd you do that for?"

"*Was is do uff?* [What's the matter here?]" His forehead wrinkled as he studied the kapp hanging in midair.

Rachel giggled as she watched the kapp sway in the gentle breeze. "It looks like you caught a big one, Grandpa!"

Grandpa's eyes twinkled and he laughed. "We won't be throwing this one back into the lake."

Rachel jumped up to retrieve her kapp. She worked to gently remove the hook, but the hook left a noticeable hole. "Oh no! You put a hole in my kapp! It's ruined now," she said with a frown.

Grandpa examined the damage to her kapp. "I'm sorry, Rachel. It was an accident. I sure didn't do it on purpose."

Rachel tossed her pole to the ground. "I don't feel like fishing anymore."

"Come on, Rachel," Grandpa said, placing a hand on her shoulder. "Let's not let a little accident ruin our wishing fishing trip."

She crossed her arms and stared straight ahead.

"Are you going to forgive me?"

Rachel shrugged. "Mom's gonna be mad when she sees that my kapp is ruined."

"I'll explain things to your mamm."

"She'll probably make me wear the kapp with a hole in it because she doesn't have time to make me a new one. She's too busy making *baby clothes*." Rachel sniffed. "After the boppli's born, Mom will be even busier than she is now. She probably won't have time to sew anything for me."

"I'm sure she'll take the time to make you a new kapp," Grandpa said. "Either that or she'll fix the hole in this kapp." Grandpa motioned to Rachel's fishing pole. "Are you going to fish or not?"

She shook her head. "I'm out of the mood."

"Suit yourself." Grandpa cast his line into the water. Rachel sat staring at the trees on the other side of the pond. So much for a fun day of wishing fishing! The only thing she was wishing for now was a kapp that didn't have a hole in it. If she had to wear her kapp with a hole in it to school on Monday morning, Jacob, Orlie, and some of the other kids would probably make fun of her.

"You've been awfully grumpy and unforgiving lately," Grandpa said. "What's the problem?"

She shrugged.

"Does it have anything to do with Mary moving to Indiana?"

"Maybe."

Grandpa took one hand off his fishing pole and touched Rachel's arm. "I realize you're having a hard time adjusting, but you shouldn't take it out on everyone. If you're not careful, you won't have any friends at all."

She grunted. "I don't need any friends."

"Jah, you do. We all need a good friend or two." Grandpa plucked a blade of grass and put it between his teeth. "If your attitude doesn't change, you might lose the friends you do have, and you certainly won't make any new ones."

"Humph!" Rachel grunted. "I could never be Audra's friend."

"Audra?"

"She's that new girl at school." Rachel clucked her tongue, the way Mom often did. "Audra and I are as different as Cuddles and Buddy. I don't think we could ever get along."

"It doesn't matter whether you like the same things or not," Grandpa said. "You can still be Audra's friend if you want to be."

I don't want to be Audra's friend, Rachel thought, but she didn't tell Grandpa that. Instead, she picked up her pole and cast her line into the water. "I guess I will fish awhile," she said.

Grandpa smiled. "That's good to hear."

It wasn't long before Rachel had a bite on her line, and she quickly reeled in a nice big fish.

"Do you need help taking the fish off the hook?" Grandpa asked.

Rachel shook her head. "I can manage." Carefully,

she removed the hook from the fish's mouth. Then she put the fish in the bucket Grandpa brought along. She baited her hook with another wiggly worm and cast her line into the water again.

In no time at all Rachel caught two more fish, but Grandpa had only caught one. He didn't seem to mind, though, as he leaned back on his elbows in the grass and lifted his face to the sun. "Ah, the Lord is good," he murmured.

Just then Rachel spotted a plump little frog leaping along the water's edge. It made her think of the day she caught two frogs in their backyard. She put them in a box and took them to church, hoping to race them after the service was over. But one of the frogs escaped from the box and made quite a scene during church. When Mom found out that Rachel was the one responsible for the leaping frog, she wasn't happy at all. In fact, she'd given Rachel extra chores to do. Right then and there Rachel had decided she would never catch another frog and bring it to church.

But I could catch a frog here at the pond and take it home with me, Rachel thought. She set her fishing pole aside and crawled slowly through the grass toward the frog.

"What are you doing, Rachel?" Grandpa asked.

"Shh. . .I'm getting ready to catch a frog." She reached out her hand, and—*flump!*—the frog leaped into the air and landed on a rock in the shallow water.

Rachel leaned out as far as she could, but she couldn't quite reach the frog.

Ribbet! Ribbet! Mr. Frog leaped onto another rock a short distance away.

Rachel knew there was only one way to catch that sneaky old frog, but she would have to move fast. She crouched down low and waited to see what the frog would do. It just sat there, still as could be.

In one quick movement, Rachel stepped into the water and thrust out her arm. Her fingers were just inches from the frog, but it leaped again. This time it landed back in the grass. *Ribbet! Ribbet!*

"I don't think that old frog wants to be caught," Grandpa said with a chuckle.

Rachel groaned and trudged through the water. She was getting ready to step out when her foot slipped on a slimy rock, and—*splash!*—into the water she went! She came up spitting and sputtering, "Trouble, trouble, trouble! All I ever have is trouble!"

Grandpa held his sides and rocked back and forth as he laughed. "Ach, Rachel, I thought you came here to fish, not take a dip in the pond."

"It's not funny, Grandpa," Rachel said as she sloshed out of the water. "My kapp's got a hole in it, and now my clothes are soaking wet. I'll be in trouble with Mom for sure."

Grandpa grabbed an old quilt from the back of his buggy and wrapped it around her shoulders. "I'm sure your mamm will understand once you explain what happened."

Rachel shook her head. "You don't know Mom like I do."

He laughed some more and slapped his knee. "She's my *dochder* [daughter], Rachel. I raised her for over nineteen years before she married your daed. I think I know her well enough."

Rachel thought about the day last summer when she fell in the pond while making a mud dam with Jacob. Mom called them out of the water, saying it was time to go home. Jacob went right away, but Rachel didn't come when she was called, choosing instead to work on her dam. Then she slipped on a slimy rock and fell into the water, just like she did today. As punishment for not coming when she was called, Rachel had to wash her dress when they got home from the picnic.

Mom will probably be mad when she sees my torn kapp and wet dress, Rachel thought as she grabbed her fishing pole and climbed into the buggy. *She'll probably give me more chores to do.*

When Rachel and Grandpa arrived home, she spotted Jacob in the yard, giving Buddy a ride in the wheelbarrow Mom used for gardening. "Jacob giving his dog a ride in the wheelbarrow is so lecherich," she said as Grandpa helped her down from the buggy.

Grandpa's forehead wrinkled. "It's no more ridiculous than you trying to catch a frog or giving Cuddles a ride on your skateboard."

I wonder if Grandpa's mad because I got three fish and he only got one, Rachel thought as she hurried across the lawn. *Maybe that's why he's sticking up for Jacob.*

When Rachel entered the house, she found Mom lying on the sofa reading a book. "I thought you were going to sew baby clothes today," Rachel said, as she stood in the doorway.

"I did get some sewing done, but I got tired and decided to rest." Mom gave a noisy yawn. "How was the fishing? Did you catch any fish?"

Rachel nodded. "I got three and Grandpa got one."

Mom chuckled but didn't look up. "I'll bet he wasn't too happy about only getting one fish."

"He said he didn't mind."

Mom sat up and stretched. "Where is Grandpa now?"

"He's outside putting the horse in the barn." Rachel removed her kapp from her head. "Grandpa snagged my kapp with his fishing hook, and now there's a hole in it," she said with a frown. "Then I fell in the pond and got my dress all wet."

"It's too bad those things happened, but it's not the end of the world. I have some extra kapps put away in a drawer, so you can have one of those. You will need to get out of your wet clothes, though."

Rachel waited to see if Mom would say anything more.

"Is there something else?" Mom asked, giving Rachel a questioning look.

Rachel shook her head. "No, I—uh—just wondered if you wanted me to wash my dress."

Mom shook her head. "I'll wash clothes on Monday morning, so just put your dress and under things in the laundry basket. Then change into some clean clothes."

"Okay, Mom." Rachel looked at her kapp again. At least she wouldn't have to wear a kapp with a hole in it to school on Monday morning. And she couldn't get over how calm Mom had seemed when she'd told her what had happened at the pond. *Maybe Grandpa does know her better than me,* she thought. *Or maybe it's because I wasn't being disobedient when I fell in the pond this time.*

Rachel turned toward the door leading to the stairs, but she'd only taken a few steps when Mom called, "Oh, Rachel, I almost forgot. There's a surprise on the table for you."

"What surprise?" Rachel loved surprises.

"A letter came for you in today's mail."

"Is—is it from Mary?"

Mom nodded.

Well, it's about time Mary wrote to me, Rachel thought.

"I got a letter from Mary's mamm, too."

Rachel started for the kitchen but halted again when Mom said, "You can get the letter now, but then you'd better go right upstairs and change out of those wet clothes."

"Okay, Mom." Rachel raced into the kitchen. Sure enough, there was a letter lying on the table. She scooped it up and rushed upstairs to her room. She placed the letter on the bed and quickly changed into a clean dress. Then she picked up the letter and flopped onto the mattress.

Rachel's hands shook as she tore the envelope open

and began to read.

> *Dear Rachel,*
>
> *I'm sorry it's taken me so long to write, but I've been awful busy since we moved. There have been boxes to unpack, things to put away, and the house to help clean.*
>
> *I like my new school. The teacher's name is Sadie, and she's real nice. Oh, and I've made a new friend. . . Betty Stutzman. She used to live in Missouri and moved here a few months before we did. Betty and I are going shopping with our* midder *[mothers] this Saturday. We'll probably go out to lunch somewhere, too.*
>
> *How are things with you? Have you taken Cuddles for any more rides on your skateboard?*
>
> *Write back soon.*
>
> *Love,*
> *Mary*

Rachel let the letter fall to the bed. She felt like she'd been kicked in the stomach by a wild horse. It wasn't fair! Mary had a new friend—and she didn't. And Mary hadn't said a word about the letter Rachel had written her. Didn't Mary even care how miserable Rachel had felt since she'd moved away?

I'm not going to write Mary back, Rachel decided. Tears welled in her eyes, and she pulled the pillow over her head. "Oh, Mary, I miss you so much. I have no friends now, and I'm so lonely."

The bed squeaked, and Rachel felt someone touch her hand. "You have to be a friend if you want to have any friends," Mom said softly.

Rachel pulled the pillow aside and sniffed. "Mary doesn't need me anymore. She's found a new friend. I wish Mary would move back to Pennsylvania so things would be like they used to be."

"I know it's hard to have your best friend move away, but you shouldn't be mad at Mary for making a new friend." Mom handed Rachel a tissue. "Don't you think it's time for you to make a new friend, too?"

Rachel sniffled and blew her nose. "I'll think about it."

Chapter 9

Bubbles and Troubles

Rachel grunted as she carried a basket of clean clothes out to the clothesline and placed it on the ground. When she arrived home from school this afternoon, Mom said she hadn't felt well this morning, so it had taken her longer than normal to get their clothes washed, and she'd only hung a few things on the line. She asked Rachel to hang the rest of the things while she went back inside to rest before it was time to start supper.

Rachel glanced at the barn. She wished she was in there riding her skateboard or playing with Cuddles instead of hanging laundry out to dry. Maybe if she hurried and got it done, there would be time for her to play before she had to help Mom with supper.

Rachel bent down, picked up a pair of grandpa's trousers, and stepped onto the wooden stool she used to help her reach the clothesline. She had just clipped the trousers to the line when Buddy ambled across the yard toward her, an old bone hanging from his mouth. She looked away in disgust, hoping the dog wouldn't notice her.

Disgusting mutt, Rachel thought as she pinned one of Mom's towels to the line. *He's nothing but trouble.*

Woof! Woof!

Rachel looked down just in time to see Buddy drop his bone at her feet, dip his head into the basket, and grab one of the towels in his mouth.

"Give me that!" she shouted.

Buddy flicked his ears, swished his tail, and darted away, dragging the towel across the grass.

Rachel hopped down from the stool and tore across the yard after him. "You come back with that towel, you bad breath, hairy beast!"

Buddy kept running—straight through the biggest patch of mud he could find!

Rachel gasped. "Look what you've done to Mom's clean towel! It's filthy!" Rachel grabbed one end of the towel, and pulled.

Buddy's whole body shook as he growled and yanked on the towel.

"You'd better let go," Rachel said through gritted teeth.

Gr-r-r-r. . . Rip! The towel tore in two!

Rachel's whole body felt angry. She shook her fists and stamped her feet at Buddy and hollered, "Mom's not gonna be happy about this!"

Woof! Woof! Buddy wagged his tail, dropped his half of the towel, and bounded back to the laundry basket.

Rachel took off after him, waving her piece of towel

in the air. "Oh no, you don't!"

But she was too late. Buddy grabbed another towel, and he ran in circles, dragging the towel across the grass, through the dirt, and into the same mud.

Rachel knew better than to grab the towel this time. Buddy would probably tear it like the last one. She turned toward the house and cupped one hand around her mouth. "Jacob Yoder, you'd better come out here right now and get your dog!"

Jacob poked his head out the back door. "What's the trouble, Rachel? Why are you yelling?"

"Buddy's the trouble! *Your* dog took a clean towel from the laundry basket, dragged it through the mud, then ripped it in two when I tried to take it from him." Rachel pointed to Buddy, who lay under the clothesline with his head resting on the second towel he'd swiped from the basket. "Now he's got another towel and is using it for a pillow!"

Jacob sprinted across the yard, grabbed Buddy's collar, and pulled him away from the towel. "There, is that better?"

Rachel shook her head. "Nothing will be better until you get rid of that nuisance! He's been nothing but trouble ever since Orlie gave him to you!"

"I think you're exaggerating," Jacob said. "Buddy's a nice dog."

She held up the dirty piece of towel in her hand. "Do you call this *nice*?"

"I don't think Buddy ripped it on purpose. He

probably thought you were playing."

"Jah, right! That dog needs to be trained, and you ought to know better than to let him run free on laundry day!"

Jacob scratched the side of his head. "I thought I had Buddy penned up. I wonder if I forgot to latch the gate on his pen."

"I'm going in the house right now to tell Mom what happened. If I get in trouble for this, it'll be your fault for not keeping Buddy penned up!"

Before Jacob had a chance to reply, Rachel raced across the yard toward the house. She'd just stepped into the kitchen when—*bam!*—she heard a loud crash followed by a rattling noise coming from the living room.

"Mom, are you okay?" Rachel hurried into the room where she found Mom on her hands and knees holding pieces of a broken jar. Dozens of marbles rolled all over the floor!

Rachel gasped. "Ach, Mom, what happened to my jar of marbles?"

Mom looked up and stared at Rachel over the top of her glasses. "I was dusting the end table and accidentally knocked the jar on the floor."

Rachel frowned. "I saved up my money to buy that special jar for my marbles and now it's broken. Why weren't you more careful when you were dusting, Mom?"

"I didn't do it on purpose," Mom said as she rose slowly to her feet. "I'm sorry your jar is broken, but if you'd put the jar of marbles away in your room like

I asked you to do this morning, this would not have happened." She pointed to the piece of towel in Rachel's hands. "What happened to that towel?"

"It's Buddy's fault." Rachel sniffed a couple of times, trying to hold back the tears clogging her throat. "He got out of his dog run and took a towel from the basket of clean clothes. When I ran after him, he sloshed the towel through mud. Then when I tried to get the towel away from him, he ripped it in two." She gulped in a quick breath of air. "When I wasn't looking, Buddy pulled another towel from the basket and laid his dirty, smelly head on it like it was a pillow. I think you should make Jacob get rid of him!"

"Do I ask Mom to get rid of you every time you do something wrong?" Jacob said as he entered the room. He looked over at Mom. "I don't think Buddy meant to get those towels dirty. I'm sure he was only playing." He glared at Rachel. "And it's *her* fault one of the towels ripped in two!"

"Were you outside when this all happened?" Mom asked Jacob.

He shook his head. "I was in the kitchen having a snack."

"You know your dog's not supposed to be out of his pen unless you're there to watch him."

Jacob stared at the floor. "I know, but I didn't let Buddy out of his pen, honest."

"How did Buddy get out?" Mom asked.

Jacob shrugged. "I don't know. Maybe he unlatched the gate."

"Right!" Rachel grunted. "Like that dumm mutt's smart enough to unlatch the gate himself."

"He's not a dumm mutt. He's very *schmaert* [smart]," Jacob said. "You're just *en aldi grauns* [an old grumbler] who likes to blame everyone for everything and doesn't know how to forgive."

Rachel's chin quivered as she glared at him. "You take that back, Jacob Yoder!"

"Why should I? It's the truth."

"A lot you know. For your information—"

Mom clapped her hands. "That's enough!" She motioned to the marbles on the floor. "Rachel, gather up all these marbles before one of us slips on them and gets hurt. After that, you can wash the towel Buddy laid his head on." She looked over at Jacob. "Go outside and make sure your dog is in his pen and that the gate's secured. I don't want any more dirty laundry to do today."

Jacob nodded and hurried out of the room. Rachel dropped to her knees and started gathering up marbles, grumbling as she put each one into an empty coffee can Mom gave her. By the time she finished, she was tired and cranky.

Maybe Jacob's right, Rachel thought as she lugged the marbles up the steps to her room. *I do feel like en aldi grauns today.*

Rachel put the marble-filled coffee can on the floor in her closet. She was tempted to sit on the bed and hold her faceless doll, but she knew Mom was waiting for her to wash the dirty towel. With a weary sigh she headed back downstairs.

When Rachel finished washing the towel in the kitchen sink, Mom smiled and said, "You're free to play until it's time to help with supper. Why don't you find something fun to do?"

"Don't you want me to hang up the rest of the laundry that's still in the basket outside?" Rachel asked.

Mom shook her head. "I'll take care of that."

"But I thought you weren't feeling well today."

"I just had a queasy stomach this morning, but I'm feeling better this afternoon." She patted Rachel's head. "I think you've done enough work for now, so I'll take over your job of hanging the clothes."

"Danki, Mom." Rachel headed out to the barn, hoping to find Cuddles there. But when she entered the barn, she saw no sign of her cat. She took a seat on a bale of straw and looked around. It was quiet in the barn. Sunbeams streamed through the cracks in the ceiling, and a pigeon cooed from the loft overhead.

Rachel yawned and closed her eyes. She was too tired to skateboard or swing on the rope hanging from the hayloft. *Maybe I'll visit with old Tom,* she decided. *He probably needs cheering up as much as I do.*

Rachel walked to the part of the barn where the horses were kept. When she came to old Tom's stall, she opened the door and peeked in. She was disappointed to see that the old horse was lying in a pile of straw, fast asleep.

"Guess I'd better find something else to do," Rachel

mumbled as she shut the stall door and headed back through the barn. She was almost to the door when she spotted a jar of bubbles on a shelf. *Maybe Grandpa would like to blow some bubbles with me,* she thought as she reached for the jar. *Grandpa makes bubbles better than anyone I know.*

Rachel hurried to the house. She found Mom in the kitchen, peeling potatoes over the kitchen sink. "Did you finish hanging the laundry already?" she asked.

Mom nodded. "Just got it done a few minutes ago."

"Is it time to start supper?" Rachel hoped she had time to play before she had to help Mom in the kitchen.

Mom pushed her glasses to the bridge of her nose and shook her head. "I'm just getting a head start on things. You go ahead and play some more if you want to."

"I'm going to sit on the back porch and blow some bubbles," Rachel said. "I came in the house to see if Grandpa wants to join me."

Mom motioned to the bedroom down the hall. "Grandpa's taking a nap right now. He spent most of the day working in the garden and said he was plumb tuckered out."

Rachel couldn't hide her disappointment as she frowned and said, "Maybe I won't blow any bubbles then."

Mom clucked her tongue noisily. "Don't martyr yourself, Rachel."

"What's 'martyr' mean?" Rachel asked.

"A martyr is a willing victim who suffers for a cause,"

Mom replied as she continued peeling potatoes. "People who martyr themselves often do it to make others feel sorry for them."

Rachel thought about that a few seconds. Was she acting like a martyr by not wanting to blow bubbles by herself?

"You've been grumpy and out of sorts ever since Mary moved away," Mom said. "I think what you need to do is go out on the porch, blow a few bubbles, and thank God for all the good things He's given you."

"Jah, okay." Rachel went out the door, took a seat on the porch step, and opened the jar of bubbles. She dipped the bubble wand inside, pulled it back out, and blew. A colorful bubble formed. When she waved the wand, the bubble sailed across the yard.

Rachel made a couple more bubbles, and was about to put the lid back on the jar, when Cuddles darted out from under the porch and pounced on a bubble that hovered just above the ground.

Rachel blew another bubble—and then another. As fast as she made each bubble, Cuddles popped it. Rachel laughed.

This is kind of fun, Rachel thought. In fact, she was actually having a good time. She hadn't laughed this much since Mary moved away.

She closed her eyes. *Dear God: Thanks for Cuddles, and bubbles, and all the good things You've given me.*

Rachel's eyes snapped open when Cuddles bounded up the steps, pranced over to the bubble jar, and—

thunk!—swatted at it with her right front paw. *Splat!*—the bubble liquid spilled out of the jar and all over the porch.

Rachel groaned. So much for a fun time of blowing bubbles!

She closed her eyes and thought about all her troubles. She had trouble with Audra, trouble with Jacob, trouble with Buddy, and now trouble with Cuddles.

She sighed deeply. *I used to have some friends, but they seem to be disappearing as fast as Cuddles popped my bubbles. I wonder if I'll ever have any friends again. I wonder if my life will always be full of popping bubbles and all kinds of troubles.*

Chapter 10

In the Doghouse

The following Saturday morning, after Rachel finished feeding the chickens, she saw a big truck pull into their yard. She figured maybe Pap had ordered some farming supplies, so she walked past the truck without paying it much attention.

"Hey, little girl," the driver said as he and another man climbed out of the truck. "Do you know where we're supposed to put this trampoline?" He jabbed his thumb toward a large cardboard box in the back of the truck.

Rachel tipped her head and looked at the box. "Trampoline?"

He nodded. "That's right. I need to know where we should set it up."

"There must be some mistake." She shook her head. "I'm sure no one here ordered a trampoline. I think you must have come to the wrong address."

The man studied the piece of paper in his hands. "Is

this the home of Levi Yoder?"

Rachel nodded.

"Then this is the right address."

Since it wasn't Christmas or anyone's birthday, Rachel was sure it was a mistake. She was about to head to the house to tell Mom about the delivery when Grandpa came out the back door, grinning from ear to ear.

"Is that the trampoline I ordered?" he asked, motioning to the back of the truck.

The deliveryman nodded. "Are you Levi Yoder?"

"No, I'm Noah Schrock. I'm the one who ordered the trampoline."

Rachel's mouth dropped open. "*You* ordered a trampoline?"

Grandpa nodded. "Sure did."

"Who—who's it for?" Rachel squeaked. "I mean, it's nobody's birthday, and it's not Christmas, so—"

"It doesn't have to be a special occasion for me to give a gift, and this gift is for everyone in the family." Grandpa pulled his fingers through his long beard and chuckled. "Well, anyone who's able to jump on the silly thing."

Rachel's heart went *thump-thump-thump!* "That would be me!" she said excitedly. "I'd love to jump on the trampoline!"

He smiled and patted the top of her head. "I figured you might."

The delivery man cleared his throat real loud. "Where do you want us to put the trampoline?"

Grandpa looked at Rachel, and Rachel shrugged. "Pap's out in the fields with Henry and Jacob. Should I go ask Mom?"

Grandpa nodded.

Rachel raced into the house. "Mom, guess what?" she hollered when she entered the kitchen where Mom sat at her sewing machine. "Grandpa bought us a trampoline!"

Mom looked up and smiled. "I knew he was going to. I just didn't know when it would arrive."

"How come you never said anything?" Rachel asked.

Mom rubbed the bridge of her nose, where her glasses were supposed to be, then she pushed them back in place. "He said he wanted it to be a surprise."

"It's a surprise, all right." Rachel's head bobbed up and down. "The deliverymen want to know where they should set up the trampoline."

Mom tapped her finger against her chin. "Let's see now. . . . Between the barn and the garden might be a good place."

"All right, I'll tell the men where you want it." Rachel raced for the door.

By the time the men had the trampoline set up, Jacob, Henry, and Pap had returned from the fields for lunch.

"Look what Grandpa bought for us." Rachel pointed to the trampoline. "I can hardly wait to try it out!"

"It's very nice," Pap said, "but you'll have to wait until after lunch to jump on it."

Rachel wished she could jump on it now, but she knew better than to argue with Pap. If she did, he might say she couldn't jump at all.

"I think I'm going to take my faceless doll to jump on the trampoline," Rachel said to Mom when lunch was over and the dishes were done.

Mom squinted at Rachel over the top of her glasses. "Do you think that's a good idea? What if the doll falls off the trampoline and lands in the dirt?"

"That won't happen because I'll be holding onto her."

Mom shrugged. "All right then. But do be careful."

"I will, Mom."

As Rachel passed the living room, she spotted Grandpa sitting in the rocking chair. His eyes were closed and soft snores came from his slightly open mouth, letting her know he was asleep.

She scampered up the stairs to her room, hurried over to her dresser, picked up the doll, and raced out of the room.

"Where's Jacob? Is he going to jump on the trampoline with me?" Rachel asked Mom when she stepped into the kitchen.

"I'm not sure what Jacob plans to do," Mom replied as she picked up a broom and started sweeping the floor. "Your daed and Henry returned to work in the fields, but I think Jacob went out to the dog run to see Buddy."

Rachel wrinkled her nose. "If he'd rather spend time with that mutt than jump on the new trampoline, that's fine with me."

"Be careful," Mom called as Rachel scurried out the door.

"I will." Rachel hurried out to the trampoline.

Using the step stool Grandpa put there before lunch, she set her doll on the trampoline and climbed up beside it. Her legs wobbled as she picked up the doll and stood. She sucked in a deep breath and held both arms out at her sides to keep her balance. She'd never been on a trampoline before, but she'd seen other children jumping on their trampolines. It didn't look so hard. She was sure she could do it.

Keeping both arms out at her sides as she held onto her doll, Rachel began to bounce slowly. Up. . .down. . . up. . .down. She picked up speed and jumped a little higher. Up. . .down. . .up. . .down. . . "*Whee*. . .this is sure fun!"

Woof! Woof! Woof!

Rachel glanced to the right and saw Jacob running across the yard with Buddy at his side. They were heading her way.

"Oh no," she mumbled. "Here comes trouble."

"Are you and your doll having fun up there, Rachel?" Jacob asked as he approached the trampoline.

She nodded and kept jumping.

Woof! Woof! Buddy stood beneath the trampoline with his mouth wide open.

"I hope you're not planning to let that dog of yours on the trampoline," Rachel said.

Jacob shook his head. "Of course not. We're just here to watch."

"Look how high I can go!" Rachel jumped so high her breath caught in her throat. Suddenly the doll snapped out of her hand. It flipped into the air, floated back down, and landed right in Buddy's mouth!

Rachel gasped.

Buddy pranced off toward his dog run with the faceless doll's body dangling from his mouth.

"Jacob, get your dog!" Rachel hollered. "He's got my doll!"

Jacob took off after Buddy, and Rachel jumped down from the trampoline and rushed after him. They found Buddy lying outside his doghouse with the doll between his paws.

Rachel gingerly picked up the doll and nearly choked on her words. "It—it's all chewed up!" She shook her finger at Buddy as tears clogged her throat. "You're a *bad dog*, and I'm very angry with you!"

Buddy looked up at her and whimpered.

"He didn't mean to do it," Jacob said. "When the doll flew off the trampoline, Buddy probably thought you were throwing him a toy to play with."

"I was *not* throwing him a toy!" Rachel scowled at Jacob and held up the mangled doll. "This is what happens when you let that flea-bitten animal run free!"

"I'm sorry," Jacob mumbled. "I didn't know Buddy would chew up your doll."

Rachel burst into tears. "Mary gave me this to remember her by, and—and now it's ruined!"

"I said I was sorry. What more can I do?"

"You can keep that dog in his pen where he belongs!"

"He can't be in there every minute of the day," Jacob said. "It wouldn't be fair."

"I suppose it's fair that my doll's chewed up?"

Jacob pointed to the doghouse and said, "In, Buddy."

Woof! Woof! Instead of going to the doghouse like he was supposed to do, Buddy jumped up and raced across the yard like his tail was on fire.

Jacob took off after the dog, waving his hands and hollering, "Come back here, Buddy! Come back here right now!"

Rachel groaned and stomped to the house. "Look what Jacob's dog did to my doll!" she wailed when she entered the kitchen and found Mom and Grandpa sitting at the table drinking tea.

Mom's mouth fell open, and Grandpa's bushy gray eyebrows shot up when they looked at the mangled doll Rachel held in her hands.

"How did Buddy get your doll?" Mom asked.

"The doll slipped when I was jumping on the trampoline, and Buddy was standing nearby with his mouth wide open." Rachel sniffed a couple of times. "The beautiful faceless doll Mary gave me landed in Buddy's mouth, and he chewed it all up! Now the doll is ruined!"

Mom pulled Rachel into her arms and gave her a hug. "As soon as I find the time, I'll make you another doll."

Rachel shook her head. "It wouldn't be the same. This doll was all I had to remember Mary. Now, thanks to Jacob's big hairy bad-breathed mutt, my doll is gone!"

"Sounds to me like Buddy's in the doghouse," said Grandpa with a shake of his head.

"No, he's not." Rachel motioned to the kitchen window. "Look out there and you'll see—Buddy's running around the yard, and Jacob's chasing after him."

"When I said Buddy was in the doghouse, I meant that he's gotten himself in trouble." Grandpa's lips curved slightly upwards. "It's an old expression that people use, Rachel."

Rachel didn't like the fact that Grandpa thought this was funny. And she didn't like Buddy or what he'd done to her doll!

"You know, Rachel," Grandpa continued, "it was your choice to take the doll outside on the trampoline."

"That's right," Mom said. "So you can't put all the blame on Jacob or his dog. If the doll hadn't fallen off the trampoline, Buddy wouldn't have run away with it and chewed it up."

Rachel frowned. She didn't understand why everyone was taking Buddy's side. It wasn't fair!

With a strangled sob, she marched across the kitchen, threw the mangled doll into the garbage can, and rushed out of the room.

Rachel entered her bedroom, flopped onto the bed, and cried into her pillow until there were no tears left. Finally she sat up, dried her eyes on a tissue, and went over to her desk. She pulled open the drawer, took out some paper and a pen, and wrote Mary a letter.

Dear Mary,

Today started out pretty good. A delivery truck came with a new trampoline Grandpa ordered for us. I thought it would be fun to hold the faceless doll you gave me while I jumped on the trampoline, but a terrible thing happened. When I did a really high bounce, the doll slipped out of my hand and Jacob's dumm dog caught the doll in his mouth. Then Buddy ran across the yard, and by the time Jacob and I got to him, the hairy mutt had chewed up the doll! Now I have nothing to remember you by.

Rachel stopped writing long enough to blow her nose. Telling Mary about the doll made her feel even sadder, but she thought Mary had a right to know what had happened.

Swallowing against the lump in her throat, Rachel continued with the letter.

I wish Jacob would get rid of Buddy. That dog's been nothing but trouble since the first day he came to live here. He chases Cuddles, doesn't come when he's called, and he likes to jump up and lick my face!

Grandpa says that when someone's in trouble, they're in the doghouse. Well, I can tell you this much—Buddy's in the doghouse with me!

Chapter 11

Skateboard Mishap

Ach, Mom, do I have to go?" Rachel groaned when she came downstairs Saturday morning. Mom said they would be visiting Audra and her mother.

Mom glanced at Rachel over the top of her glasses. "I think you need to go and make peace with Audra, don't you?"

Rachel frowned. "I don't see why. Audra doesn't like me, and I don't like her."

"Be that as it may," Mom said as she moved to the stove, "when I met Naomi at the store the other day, she invited us to visit at their place today, so we're going."

Rachel was tempted to argue, but she knew once Mom had made up her mind about something, there was no changing it. Feeling like something heavy rested on her shoulders, she began setting the table for breakfast.

"How come you're wearing such a big frown on your face this morning, Rachel?" Jacob asked when he entered the kitchen a few minutes later.

"I'm not frowning," she mumbled as she placed the

glasses on the table.

"Jah, you are."

"Am not."

He nudged her arm. "Then how come there's a row of tiny wrinkles on your forehead?"

Rachel reached up and touched her forehead. Jacob was right—there were some wrinkles there.

Jacob went to the sink and turned on the water to wash his hands. "So how come you're frowning, Rachel?"

"She's upset because she and I are going over to the Burkholders' house after breakfast," Mom said before Rachel could reply.

"Mom wants me to make peace with Audra," Rachel muttered.

"I think that's a good idea," Jacob said. "While you're at it, why don't you stop by Buddy's doghouse and make peace with him?"

Rachel whirled around and scowled at Jacob. "I'll never make peace with your dog. He's nothing but trouble!"

"You're nothing but trouble," Jacob shot back.

"No, you're bigger tr—"

Mom clapped her hands. "That's enough! I get tired of you two bickering all the time. It's certainly not pleasing to God."

Rachel's cheeks heated up. She didn't like it when Mom scolded her—even when she knew she was wrong.

"You're awfully quiet," Mom said as she and Rachel traveled down the road in one of Pap's buggies.

Rachel shrugged. "There's not much to say."

"What's new at school?"

"Nothing much. It's the same old thing day after day."

"Are you looking forward to summer break coming soon?"

"I guess so."

"Grandpa's looking forward to building his new greenhouse."

Rachel perked up at the mention of Grandpa's greenhouse. "Grandpa said I might be able to help in the greenhouse whenever I'm not in school."

"That would be nice." Mom reached across the seat and touched Rachel's arm. "Of course, you won't be able to work in the greenhouse all the time. There will be chores at the house to do, and after the boppli comes I'll need your help even more for a while."

Rachel frowned. She didn't like the idea of having more chores to do. She wasn't sure she liked the idea of Mom having a baby, either. But then, there wasn't much she could do about that. She just hoped she'd be able to spend plenty of time with Grandpa in his greenhouse. She was sure working around all those flowers would be a lot of fun.

"Here we are," Mom said as she guided their horse and buggy onto the Burkholders' driveway.

Rachel spotted Audra's mother sitting in a chair on the front porch, but there was no sign of Audra. *Good. Maybe Audra's not here today. Maybe she went to visit Orlie or something.*

Mom stopped the buggy in front of the hitching rail

near the barn and climbed down. Rachel did the same.

"I'm glad you were able to come," Naomi said when Mom and Rachel joined her on the porch. She turned to Rachel and smiled. "Audra's in the barn playing. Would you like to join her?"

Rachel forced a smile to her lips and said what she knew Mom expected her to say: "Jah, sure." She left the porch and walked slowly to the barn.

She found Audra sitting on a bale of straw, fiddling with the string on a wooden yo-yo.

"Jacob has one of those," Rachel said, "but he doesn't play with it much anymore." She sighed. "He'd rather play with his dog."

Audra grunted. "My older bruder Jared made this for me, but I may never get to play with it if I can't get the string untangled."

"Want me to try?" Rachel offered.

"Jah, sure, if you think you can." Audra handed the yo-yo to Rachel.

As Rachel worked on untangling the string, Audra hummed and tapped her foot.

Rachel gritted her teeth as she struggled with the yo-yo string. It really was a mess!

"If you can't get it, that's okay," Audra said. "I don't need to play with the yo-yo right now."

"I'm sure I can get it. Just give me a few more minutes." Rachel fiddled with the string a while longer and finally gave up. "Why don't we do something else?" she suggested, setting the yo-yo aside. "I don't like to play with yo-yos that much anyway."

"Do you know how to skateboard?" Audra asked.

"Jah, sure," Rachel said with a nod.

"Maybe you'd like to try out the new skateboard ramp Jared made."

"You have your own skateboard ramp?"

"Actually, it belongs to both me and Brian. We take turns using it," Audra said.

"The only place I have to skateboard is the concrete floor of our barn—when it's not full of hay, that is," Rachel said. "It would be wunderbaar to have a ramp of my own to skateboard on."

Audra nodded. "Jared built the ramp at the back of the barn. Let's go there now, shall we?"

"Okay."

Audra led the way, and Rachel followed. They'd only gone a few steps, when Audra halted and shrieked. "Eeeeek!"

"What's the matter?" Rachel asked. "Why are you yelling?"

"I almost ran into that!" Audra pointed to a long-legged spider inside a lacy web. "I hate spiders!"

"It's not moving. Maybe it's dead." Rachel couldn't imagine why Audra would be scared of a little old spider.

Audra shivered. "I sure hope so."

"There's only one way to find out." Rachel grabbed a piece of straw and poked the spider gently. The spider wiggled its legs.

"It's definitely *not* dead," Rachel said.

"Yuck!" Audra scrunched up her nose. "How could you touch that horrible thing?"

"It was easy." Rachel shrugged. "Unless some dirty insect lands on my food, bugs don't bother me at all."

"I think all bugs are disgusting!" Audra ducked under the spider web. "That's where we skateboard." She pointed to the wooden ramp that had been set up near the back of the barn.

As Rachel stared at it, she felt envious. Why couldn't she have a ramp like that to skate on? Maybe she would ask Pap or Henry to build one for her next birthday.

"Here's my skateboard." Audra picked up the wooden skateboard sitting on the floor near the ramp. "Jared made this for me, too."

"If I'd known you had a place to skateboard, I would have brought my skateboard with me today," Rachel said. "My brothers gave me a skateboard for my birthday last year."

"We can take turns using mine," Audra said.

"Really? You'd let me use your skateboard?"

"Sure, why not?" Audra handed the skateboard to Rachel. "I'll even let you go first."

Rachel was surprised at how nice Audra was being. Maybe the two of them could be friends after all. She smiled and took the skateboard from Audra. "Danki."

Rachel stepped onto the skateboard and skated back and forth across the floor a few times. Then, pushing off as fast as she could, she headed for the ramp. "*Whee. . . this is so much fun!*" She skated up one side of the ramp and down the other.

"It's my turn now," Audra said.

"Just one more time." Rachel got the skateboard going good, and up the ramp she went. "Watch this, Audra." Leaning to one side, Rachel swerved back and forth, tipped the skateboard with the heel of her foot, and sailed down the other side.

She was almost to the bottom of the ramp when—*floop!*—the back wheel of the skateboard dropped off the edge of the ramp. Rachel's foot slipped, too, and the skateboard flew into the air and landed on the floor with a *thud*.

"Ach, my skateboard—you've ruined it!" Audra hollered.

Rachel went weak in the knees when she saw that the skateboard had broken into two pieces. "I'm sorry. I didn't expect that to happen," she stammered.

Audra's lower lip jutted out and she stamped her foot. "I think you did that on purpose."

Rachel shook her head. "Why would I do that?"

"Maybe to get even with me for mixing up our lunch pails at school. Or maybe you're still mad about the mud I splattered on your dress, or the baseball that hit you in the nose, or the nosebleed you got when I accidentally tripped you at school." Audra's forehead wrinkled as she squinted at Rachel. "You haven't liked me since my first day of school!"

"I wasn't trying to get even with you—honest." Rachel swallowed around the lump in her throat. It was bad enough that Audra wouldn't accept her apology, but she was also worried that she'd be in trouble with Mom for breaking Audra's skateboard.

"I still think you broke my skateboard on purpose." Audra's eyes filled with tears. "I'm glad you're not my friend, Rachel. I don't want a friend like you!"

"Fine. If you won't accept my apology, I'm going home!" Rachel rushed out of the barn and stomped onto the Burkholders' porch where Mom sat visiting with Naomi. "I want to go home," she announced.

"Naomi and I aren't done visiting yet," Mom said. "Why don't you go back to the barn and play?"

"I can't."

"Why not?"

"I accidentally broke Audra's skateboard, and—" Rachel blinked against stinging tears and sniffed a couple of times. "I apologized to Audra, but she refuses to forgive me. She thinks I broke her skateboard on purpose."

Before either Mom or Naomi could reply, Audra showed up, holding the two pieces of her skateboard. "Look what Rachel did!" She looked at Rachel and scowled. "I'm sure she did it on purpose because she doesn't like me."

"Is that true?" Mom asked, touching Rachel's shoulder.

Rachel shook her head. "No, it's not. Audra said I could use her skateboard. When I was skating down the ramp, one of the back wheels slipped off. Then my foot slipped and I—I lost my balance." She paused and swiped at the tears rolling down her cheeks. "The skateboard sailed out from under me, flipped into the air, and broke in two pieces when it landed on the floor."

"Sounds like an accident to me," Naomi said, looking at Audra.

"No, it wasn't. Rachel broke it on purpose!" Audra jerked open the screen door and dashed into the house.

"I'll see that Rachel saves up her money and buys Audra a new skateboard," Mom said.

Naomi shook her head. "That's not necessary. I'm sure Jared will make Audra another skateboard."

Mom looked back at Rachel, as though hoping she might say something, but Rachel turned away. "I'll be out in the buggy waiting for you," she mumbled.

"I'll be there as soon as I finish my tea," Mom said.

As Rachel walked away, she heard Mom say to Naomi, "I'm sorry this happened. I had hoped Audra and Rachel would become friends."

"Jah," Naomi replied. "Our move to Pennsylvania has been hard on Audra, and I was hoping she would make new friends right away."

"I wish our girls could see how much they need each other and that they could be good friends if they would only try," Mom said.

I could never be friends with someone who won't accept my apology, Rachel thought as she hurried toward the buggy.

Chapter 12

Change of Heart

As Rachel and Mom traveled home from the Burkholders', Rachel leaned back and closed her eyes. All she could think about was the skateboard she'd broken. It wasn't fair that Audra had refused to accept her apology, or that she'd thought Rachel had broken the skateboard on purpose.

"Are you sleeping, Rachel?" Mom asked.

Rachel's eyes snapped open. "No, I was just thinking."

"About Audra's skateboard?"

"Jah."

"Don't you think it would be nice if you bought her a new skateboard?"

"Audra's mamm said I didn't have to. She said Jared would make Audra another skateboard when he found the time."

"That's true, but Jared's very busy helping his daed in the buggy shop right now. It could be quite awhile before he has the time to make a skateboard for Audra," Mom said.

Rachel frowned. "New skateboards cost a lot of money, and I only have a few quarters in my piggy bank."

"Maybe you could do some odd jobs or paint more of your ladybug rocks to sell at Kauffman's store."

"Even if I did that, it would take a long time before I had enough money to buy a new skateboard." Rachel remembered how last year she put a skateboard in layaway at Kauffman's. She sold several painted rocks, hoping to get the skateboard out of layaway in time for her birthday, but didn't come up with enough money in time. After Jacob and Henry gave her a homemade skateboard, she took the fancy store-bought skateboard out of layaway and used the money she made on something else.

Mom reached across the seat and patted Rachel's hand. "You think about it, okay?"

Rachel nodded.

When they arrived home, Rachel spotted Jacob's dog chasing her cat across the front yard. "Oh no," she moaned. "It looks like Cuddles is in trouble again."

Rachel jumped out of the buggy and sprinted across the yard. "Stop, Buddy!" she shouted. "Stop chasing Cuddles!"

Woof! Woof! Buddy kept running as he nipped at Cuddles's tail.

Me-ow! Cuddles shrieked and tore off in the

direction of the creek. Buddy followed, and Rachel raced after him.

Just as the water came into the view, the unthinkable happened. *Splat!*—Rachel's cat jumped into the creek!

Rachel gasped. "Cuddles!"

Meow! Meow! Cuddles splashed around in the water, her little head bobbing up and down.

"Hang on, Cuddles! I'm coming!" Rachel raced for the creek, but before she could put one foot in the water, Buddy leaped in, grabbed Cuddles by the scruff of the neck, and hauled her out of the water. He set the cat on the ground, and—*slurp, slurp*—licked her waterlogged head with his big red tongue.

Meow! Cuddles swiped her little pink tongue across Buddy's paw and began to purr.

Rachel's jaw dropped. She could hardly believe what she was seeing. Even though Buddy and Cuddles were complete opposites, they'd actually become friends.

I wonder if there's a way Audra and I could become friends, Rachel thought. Audra's mother said that Audra needed a friend. The truth was Rachel needed a friend, too. But she knew in order for that to happen, she would have to do something to make Audra want to be her friend. She also knew she would never make any new friends or keep the ones she had if she didn't learn to forgive.

"I've been doing the same thing to everyone else as Audra did to me today," Rachel whispered as she bent to pick up her cat. "I've refused to accept anyone's apology. I've even held grudges against my friends and family for everything they've done to hurt me—even when it was an accident."

Rachel bowed her head and closed her eyes. *Dear God,* she silently prayed, *I've been angry with everyone because Mary moved away, and I didn't see that I could keep Mary as a friend and make new friends, too. Forgive me for not forgiving. Please show me what to do to make things better between Audra and me.*

Rachel had just opened her eyes when an idea popped into her head. She knew just what she needed to do!

She picked up her cat, called Buddy to follow, and started for home, singing the little song Mom taught her about making friends: "Make new friends but keep the old. One is silver and the other gold."

Rachel was halfway to the house when Jacob came running across the field. "Mom said Buddy was chasing Cuddles and you took off after them. Is everything all right?"

Rachel nodded. "It is now."

"What happened?"

"Cuddles got into the creek, and I was afraid she might drown." Rachel looked down at Jacob's dog and patted the top of his head. "Buddy jumped in the water and rescued Cuddles. I think they've become friends."

Jacob smiled and reached over to pet Cuddles behind her ear. "I'll bet they've been friends the whole time, Rachel. I think Buddy only chases after Cuddles because he likes her and wants to play."

Woof! Woof! Buddy jumped up, put his big paws on

Rachel's chest, and—*slurp, slurp*—kissed her right on the nose.

"Get down, Buddy!" Rachel pushed him down with her knee. "I'm glad you saved Cuddles from drowning, and it's good that the two of you are friends, but I still don't appreciate your sloppy kisses."

Jacob chuckled. "I've told you before. . .Buddy licks your face because he likes you, Rachel."

Rachel wiped her nose with the back of her hand. "Jah, well, I might like him, too, if he would stop licking me."

Woof! Woof! Woof! Buddy looked up at Cuddles and wagged his tail.

Meow! Cuddles leaped from Rachel's arm and took off after Buddy.

"Now that's sure a switch. Instead of Buddy chasing Cuddles, she's chasing after him!" Jacob laughed so hard he doubled over and held his sides.

Rachel laughed, too. She ran the rest of the way home, singing at the top of her lungs, "Make new friends but keep the old. One is silver and the other gold!"

When Rachel sat around the table having lunch with her family that afternoon, she was so excited she could hardly stay in her chair. She'd come up with an idea and had gotten Mom's permission to go over to Audra's again after lunch. Henry had agreed to drive Rachel there, since he was going that way to see his girlfriend. Then Grandpa would pick Rachel up a few hours later.

Quit *rutschich* [squirming], and eat your lunch,

Rachel," Mom said, pointing to the peanut butter and jelly sandwich on Rachel's plate.

"I'm sorry. I'm just anxious to go."

Henry chuckled. "You can't go until I'm ready, and I'm not done eating yet."

Rachel picked up her sandwich and took a big bite. By the time she'd finished eating it, Henry was done with his sandwich, too.

"I'll be outside hitching my horse to the buggy," he said, pushing away from the table. "Come on out when you're ready, Rachel."

"Before you go, I'd like to say something—to you and the rest of the family."

"What is it, Rachel?" Mom asked.

"I—uh—" Rachel fiddled with the napkin in her lap. "I'm sorry for the way I've been acting since Mary moved away. I know it wasn't right to blame everyone for all the bad things that happened to me. I should have forgiven when someone said 'I'm sorry.' "

Grandpa reached over and took Rachel's hand. "I accept your apology."

"Me, too," said Mom, Pap, Henry, and Jacob.

Rachel was glad she had such a loving, forgiving family. She smiled at Henry.

"I'll come outside as soon as I've helped Mom with the dishes."

"I think Jacob can help me do the dishes today," Mom said as Henry went out the door.

"What?" Jacob's mouth dropped open. "Washing

dishes is women's work!"

"No it's not," said Pap as he scooped up his plate. "Before you kinner came along I used to help your mamm do the dishes almost every night." He wiggled his eyebrows playfully. "I kind of liked sloshing those dishes around in the soapy water. Made me feel good to see them get nice and clean."

Mom looked over at Pap and smiled. "That's right, you sure did."

Pap grinned.

Jacob rolled his eyes, and Rachel snickered. Then she picked up her dishes and took them over to the sink. "I'm heading out to the barn to get what I need to take to Audra's house," she said. "Maybe by then Henry will have his horse and buggy ready to go."

"I'll come over to the Burkholders' to get you in two hours," Grandpa said.

"Danki," Rachel called as she raced out the door.

As Rachel sat beside Henry in his buggy, she squirmed and glanced at the box sitting at her feet. After she'd put her gift to Audra in the box, she taped it shut and tied a red bow on the top so it would look like a present. She hoped Audra would accept the gift.

"You look kind of *naerfich* [nervous], Rachel," Henry said. "Are you worried Audra won't like your present?"

"A little," she admitted.

He reached across the seat and touched her arm. "Don't worry. I'm sure she'll like it just fine."

Rachel remained quiet for the rest of the trip, listening to the steady *clip-clop* of the horse's hooves and the whir from the engines as cars whizzed by.

Finally Henry pulled on the reins and directed the horse up the Burkholders' driveway. He stopped the buggy when they reached the barn, and Rachel climbed down. She lifted out the box that had been sitting on the floor. "Danki for the ride, Henry."

"You're welcome. When you get back home, tell Mom I'll be there in time for supper. See you later, Rachel." Henry lifted his hand in a wave, turned the buggy around, and headed down the driveway.

Drawing in a deep breath for courage, Rachel headed for Audra's house. When she stepped onto the porch, she set the box on the floor and knocked on the door. A few seconds later, Audra's mother answered.

"Rachel, I'm surprised to see you here again today." Naomi looked around. "Is your mamm with you?"

Rachel shook her head. "My brother, Henry, gave me a ride, and Grandpa will pick me up in a couple hours. I came to see Audra." She motioned to the box. "I have something I want to give her."

Naomi opened the door and called, "Audra, someone's here to see you."

A few moments later, Audra peeked her head around the door. She frowned when she saw Rachel. "What's *she* doing here?"

"I brought you something," Rachel said.

Audra's forehead wrinkled and she stepped through

the doorway. "What is it?"

Rachel picked up the box and handed it to Audra. "Why don't you open it and see for yourself?"

Audra placed the box on the small table near the door and removed the ribbon. Then she tore the tape off the box, lifted the flaps, and peered inside. "It's a skateboard!"

"It's the skateboard my brothers made for my birthday last year," Rachel explained. "It's to replace your broken skateboard."

"No, Rachel," Naomi said. "You can't give away one of your birthday presents. Especially since your brothers made it."

"It's okay," Rachel said. "I asked Henry and Jacob first, and they both said the skateboard is mine and I can do whatever I want with it." She smiled at Audra. "I want you to have it."

Audra's eyes widened as she lifted the skateboard out of the box. "Danki, Rachel."

"You're welcome."

"You can come over anytime you want and use the skateboard," Audra said.

Rachel smiled. "I'd like that, but there's something else I'd like even more."

"What's that?" Audra asked.

"I'd like you to be my friend."

"I'd like that, too." Audra motioned to the house. "Would you like to go up to my room and play?"

Rachel nodded.

Audra led the way, and Rachel followed her into the house.

When they entered Audra's room, Audra turned to Rachel and said, "Why don't you take a seat on the bed while I get something from my closet?"

"Okay."

When Audra returned, she held a faceless doll in her hands. "This is to replace the one Jacob's dog chewed up," she said, handing it to Rachel.

Rachel's mouth dropped open. "You—you know about that?"

Audra nodded. "I heard Jacob telling Orlie about it during recess one day."

Rachel hardly knew what to say. "Are you sure you want to give me your doll?"

"I'm very sure." Audra took a seat on the bed beside Rachel. "Whenever you come here to play we can take turns riding my new skateboard." She patted the top of the doll's head. "And when I come to your house, we can take turns playing with your new faceless doll."

"You can jump on our new trampoline when you come over to my house," Rachel said. "And I promise not to take my new faceless doll out to the trampoline when we jump."

Audra giggled. "No, that wouldn't be a good idea at all."

Rachel smiled as she thought about the verse of scripture from Ecclesiastes 4:9–10, about two being better than one. From then on, Rachel would try to remember to be kind and forgiving. She was glad she'd finally found a new friend, for she and Audra had both been given the chance for a new beginning.

Color and cut out your own faceless doll—just like Rachel's!

Other books by Wanda E. Brunstetter

Children's Fiction

Rachel Yoder—Always Trouble Somewhere Series
The Wisdom of Solomon

Adult Fiction

Sisters of Holmes County Series
Brides of Webster County Series
Daughters of Lancaster County Series
Brides of Lancaster County Series
White Christmas Pie

Nonfiction

Wanda E. Brunstetter's Amish Friends Cookbook
The Simple Life

Also available from Barbour Publishing

School's Out!

RACHEL YODER—
Always Trouble Somewhere
Book 1
by Wanda E. Brunstetter
ISBN 978-1-59789-233-9

Back to School

RACHEL YODER—
Always Trouble Somewhere
Book 2
by Wanda E. Brunstetter
ISBN 978-1-59789-234-6

Out of Control

RACHEL YODER—
Always Trouble Somewhere
Book 3
by Wanda E. Brunstetter
ISBN 978-1-59789-897-3

New Beginnings

RACHEL YODER—
Always Trouble Somewhere
Book 4
by Wanda E. Brunstetter
ISBN 978-1-59789-898-0

A Happy Heart

RACHEL YODER—
Always Trouble Somewhere
Book 5
by Wanda E. Brunstetter
ISBN 978-1-60260-134-5

Just Plain Foolishness

RACHEL YODER—
Always Trouble Somewhere
Book 6
by Wanda E. Brunstetter
ISBN 978-1-60260-135-2